MOUNTAIN GHOST STORIES AND CURIOUS TALES OF WESTERN NORTH CAROLINA

T0062077

MOUNTAIN GHOST STORIES

AND CURIOUS TALES OF WESTERN NORTH CAROLINA

by
Randy Russell and Janet Barnett

Legacy Press:

John F. Blair, Publisher
Winston-Salem, North Carolina

BLAIR

BLAIR

Durham, North Carolina

Library of Congress Cataloging-in-Publication Data

Russell, Randy.
   Mountain ghost stories and curious tales of western
North Carolina.

   1. Ghosts—North Carolina. 2. Witchcraft—North
Carolina. 3. Ghosts—Appalachian Mountains.
4. Witchcraft—Appalachian Mountains. I. Barnett,
Janet. II. Title.
BF1472.U6R87 1988   133.1'09756   88-19380
ISBN 0-89587-064-9

Paperback ISBN: 9781949467987

Cover design by Debra L. Hampton

For our parents—for all the right reasons (including our love).

And with special thanks to Carolyn Sakowski and Alton Franklin.

CONTENTS

Introduction • *ix*

Dead Dan's Shadow on the Wall • *3*
A Mountain That Talks Back • *8*
The Magic That Brought Back Tobacco • *13*
Ghosts and Gold in a World of Water and Stone • *20*
Hannibal Heaton Hears a Hoot • *27*
The Wicked Witch of Nantahala • *31*
X Marks the Spot • *39*
An Unread Letter from the Ancient Past • *47*
Bigfoot of the Balsams • *54*
Fairy Crosses and the Immortal Nunnehi • *58*
Ulagu, the Giant Yellow Jacket • *65*
The Enchanted Lake of the Smoky Mountains • *68*
The Murdered Hermit • *73*
The Phantom Choir of the Roan • *77*
Till Death Do You Part • *83*
Culgee Watson's Sunday Clothes • *88*
Belinda and the Brown Mountain Lights • *93*
A Lover Lives to Leap Again • *102*

INTRODUCTION

T he stories contained in this book have one important thing in
common, an intimate association with a particular place. It is our
goal that these tales serve to enrich one's own association with
that place, whether visiting the mountains of western North
Carolina, remembering them, or taking up residence among their
rocky valleys and forested peaks. Many faraway lives are represented there, but each life can still be felt by stepping out of a car
and placing a hand upon a tree or a foot upon a trail, or by pausing
briefly in the fragrant morning or evening air at a scenic overlook
among these magical mountains.

And the mountains *are* magic, as magic as they are real, as real
as the people who live there and who once lived there.

These tales make up what we like to think of as *real* stories of
the mountains. Ghosts and visions and witches are real? Yes. Each
tale in this book can be documented, documented as having been
told as well as having been believed. Some have been documented
either as scientific fact or as occurrences beyond the reach of
scientific fact. Each tale has survived numerous changes and
retellings, as the mountains and the people themselves have
survived and changed.

It is not our goal to provide mere word pictures of the mountains, as one might photograph their unique sizes and shapes. A photograph cannot capture a mountain, because a mountain is alive and moving. We hope, rather, that these stories contain a heartbeat of the mountains, a heartbeat echoing from times past, a heartbeat alive now as we walk, watching and listening, under the towering forests of western North Carolina.

Randy Russell and Janet Barnett

MOUNTAIN GHOST STORIES
AND CURIOUS TALES OF
WESTERN NORTH CAROLINA

DEAD DAN'S SHADOW ON THE WALL
· · · · · · · · · · · · · ·
· ·

D aniel Keith, a mountain of a man, never said a word after he was hanged.

And no one reported seeing his ghost. No mysterious lights appeared in upper-story windows and no phantom bells were heard upon the wind in Rutherfordton, North Carolina. But the soul of an innocent man cast a long shadow, a shadow that could be seen through the years.

Rutherfordton, about seventeen miles east of Lake Lure on U.S. Highway 74, was the seat of Rutherford County at a time in North Carolina's history when corporal punishment was carried out in public, at a time when many men and women were convicted of felonious acts on less evidence than is today required even to bring a case to trial.

Nobody on the jury hearing the trial of Daniel Keith believed a word he said on November 9, 1880, at the county courthouse in Rutherfordton.

A child had been murdered. An eight-year-old girl's body had been found the previous February. It was the sort of brutal murder that caused the citizens' lust for justice to overtake their reason. The girl had been beaten to death with a rock, her head repeatedly pounded until no life was left in her frail, bloodied body.

Someone reported seeing Daniel Keith near the child's home on the day of her gruesome murder. Witnesses testified that he had been drinking that day. It was enough to send the sheriff to old Dan's house that same night.

According to the sheriff, one N. E. Walker, old Dan was sober. Dan claimed no knowledge of the girl's ghastly demise, yet Sheriff Walker found a bloodstained shirt on the back porch of his house. Dan protested that the shirt was merely one he'd worn while cleaning rabbits, but he was arrested for the grisly murder all the same. He came quietly with Sheriff Walker, certain that his innocence would eventually be proven.

Perhaps the good people of Rutherfordton believed such a brutal crime could have been committed only by a brute of a man, and Daniel Keith was definitely that. By all accounts he was huge, with large, red-complected hands, the type of hands you could imagine lifting a rock over a child's small head. Dan wore a thick red beard over a ruddy face and towered above the other menfolk of Rutherford County. Many people believed it was his size alone that caused Dan to be suspected as the murderer.

As the days turned into weeks, passersby often reported that they heard angry shouts from the jail where Dan was being held in a cell against the south wall. Big Dan was questioned again and again in an attempt to elicit a confession.

Throughout the months between his arrest and trial, however, he continued to maintain his innocence as he had on the day of his arrest.

"I have kilt nobody," he vowed. "And them what say I did will pay the devil every day for saying it."

As the trial commenced, Daniel Keith was tried simultaneously on the street corners of Rutherfordton, where townspeople gathered to angrily reaffirm his obvious guilt. Popular opinion held that they shouldn't even waste time trying a man who would kill a helpless little girl with a rock.

Inside the courtroom, Dan wore a homespun, bright green shirt with wooden buttons and a grim expression of utter disbelief.

The trial was not a lengthy one. A number of townspeople testified against Daniel Keith. One sixteen-year-old lad swore that he heard the little girl scream and that he saw Dan lumbering away from the area soon afterwards—with blood dripping from his hands. However, the shirt the boy said Daniel Keith was wearing wasn't the same color as the bloodied shirt found on the big man's back porch. Most people believed the boy was fabricating a tale, seeking status by playing up to the outrage of the citizenry. Still, his testimony was allowed to stand.

In the witness chair, Daniel Keith continued to claim his innocence. His voice was said to be so strong that it was heard clearly across the street from the courthouse.

The gentlemen of the jury (no woman sat on a jury in the 1880s in North Carolina) were told by the prosecutor that Daniel Keith was a monster, a beast. And they were told there was only one way that the women and children of the community could be protected from the brutality of a creature like big Dan.

Less than an hour's recess was required for the jury to deliberate, and the court was reconvened to hear the verdict. He was found guilty as charged.

Daniel Keith was permitted to speak before the court's sentence was pronounced. Looking from juror to juror and seeking out the smug faces of the witnesses who'd testified against him, he repeated his threat.

"Those who say I kilt anybody are liars," he proclaimed. "And each of you will be hainted every day for the rest of your life. Then the devil will have ye."

Daniel Keith was sentenced to be hanged until dead between 10:00 A.M. and 2:00 P.M. on December 11. The judge further ordered all of Dan's property, down to the flour and sugar in his cupboard, to be sold at auction to help pay for the cost of the trial.

It was a cold morning when the crowds gathered from neighboring towns and counties to see justice carried out against the monster of Rutherfordton. Buggies and wagons lined the street as the death cart, a horse-drawn wagon, slowly rolled old Dan through the throng of onlookers on his way to the gallows.

Sitting between Sheriff Walker and his deputy in the wagon, Daniel Keith remained calm. Before the black sack was placed over his head, before the noose was tightened around his thick, ruddy neck, the condemned was permitted to speak his final words. "The soul of an innocent man don't rest," he said. Tears ran down his face, causing his luxuriant red beard to glisten in the cold December sun.

At one o'clock, Daniel Keith was hanged.

When a man is hanged in winter, it is said that the final dried leaves of autumn fall from the surrounding trees. What curled, brittle leaves floated to the ground that day is not recorded. The crowd dispersed. Families returned to their homes. Talk about the hanging died down as dusk descended and the body of Daniel Keith was lowered from the gallows and placed into the death cart that had brought him there.

Besides, there was something entirely new to talk about. A shadow had appeared on the outside of the south wall of the jail, a shadow that remained throughout the night and the next day as well. It was the outline of a hanged man, a big man dangling from a rope.

The shadow appeared to be permanent. People from the countryside who'd witnessed the hanging returned to Rutherfordton to view the shadow, and it was widely agreed that it must be a "haint." It would take a man as large as old Dan himself to cast such a sizable shadow, someone said.

So many people traveled to Rutherfordton to see the shadow that clung to the south wall of the jail that it became an embarrassment for the town. County employees attempted to scrub the shadow from the wall. The persistent scrubbing cleaned the paint off the wood, and still the shadow of the hanged man remained. Then the wall was painted, and additional coats were slapped upon the first. But still the shadow lingered, so clear that it could be seen at night.

The jail was sold and made into a private home. People traveling to Rutherfordton continued to ask about the wall. In a final attempt to mask the shadow of Daniel Keith, the new owner planted ivy that eventually covered the south wall. The shadow remained under the ivy, however, haunting those who'd witnessed against Daniel Keith and those who'd judged him guilty of the heinous murder of the little girl, haunting them just as he'd promised.

In 1949, two things occurred in Rutherfordton that ended the story of Daniel Keith and the shadow upon the wall.

The former jail was converted again, this time into an office building. The remodeling process included tearing down the thick ivy and adding several coats of paint to the south wall. This time the shadow did not return.

There were people in Rutherfordton who made note of another curious happenstance. An eighty-five-year-old man who lived in a home for the aged passed away. His name is not important. What is important is that this lifelong resident of Rutherfordton was the same sixteen-year-old boy who'd testified against Daniel Keith during the trial in November of 1880. And he was the last of those cursed by big Dan to die.

A Mountain
That Talks Back

On the eastern edge of the Blue Ridge Mountains is a view that looks directly back at you; it's been known to talk back, too.

Along U.S. Highway 74 through Hickory Nut Gap, automobiles follow the general route of explorer Hernando De Soto on his march through the Appalachians in search of gold and other precious metals. The highway now skirts the edge of Lake Lure, but before it was moved in the 1920s it passed directly in front of the Logan House, a historic landmark of the region. The Logan House was the first overnight stop out of Asheville along the Asheville–Rutherfordton–Charlotte stagecoach line, which operated long before the War Between the States.

The Logan House was a popular summer resort and inn as well as an overnight stop for travelers. Daily hiking parties were organized from the first sign of laurel blossoms in the spring through the colorful turning of leaves in autumn. The inn was particularly prized for its wide veranda, where guests dressed up to enjoy cold drinks. Ladies in their finest hats flirted by manipulating their decorative hand-held fans with the finesse of hummingbirds. Buttoned shoes tapped in time to the music of local fiddlers playing favorite mountain tunes. Being good company was a social grace to which many of the day aspired.

The view from the veranda featured a long mountain range towering over Lake Lure. Rumbling Bald Mountain was particularly prominent, and many guests remarked that the face of a man seemed to be etched into the side of the mountain. Unlike the profile of the old man on Grandfather Mountain, however, this face looked directly back at you. The staring face gave some guests of delicate constitution a bad case of the jitters. Someone on the summer veranda was bound to tell the story of the bad brothers of Rumbling Bald.

According to tradition, a family known for men with the size and strength of giants lived at the foot of the mountain. Rumored to be as tall as ten feet, the father and his sons were in constant, violent disagreement. They fought with each other at any time of the day or night. Because of their great size and strength, they were as good at taking a blow as dealing one out. They'd beat and wrestle each other until they were covered with bruises and blood and until exhaustion forced them to call it a draw and wait for another time to continue the fight.

One son, it seemed, fought more frequently than the others. He was the black sheep, if such a family can be said to have only one. He and his father were known to have threatened each other's lives during the heat of battle.

The family was traveling to a nearby logrolling contest one morning when the black sheep and his father got into it again and began slamming each other to the ground along the road. The remaining sons didn't try to separate the two, but continued, saving their strength for the contest. At their backs they could hear the shouts of the two big men and the thunder of bodies being tossed among the trees.

On reaching home that evening, the other sons discovered that neither their father nor brother was at home. A search was begun the next day, a search that lasted for weeks. The entire countryside was searched, but no trace was ever found.

Years passed. Their mother died of old age, and the remaining sons grew old and fathered families themselves. Then a letter was received unexpectedly. It pleaded with the brothers, now grandfathers, to come at once to a town in the Smoky Mountains to the west. They traveled to the place and discovered their missing brother on his deathbed. He confessed the happenings of that day they'd seen him last.

"We went on fightin' hard," he told the gathered men. "Rollin' and gettin' away and hittin' again, we made our way to the cleared land and this time I was 'bout to lose the fight. My mouth was cut real bad and I had broke one of my hands when Daddy ducked and I slugged a tree. The tree cracked in half and fell," the old man said, coughing up a laugh.

"He'd knock me down and I'd roll away," he said. "Then he'd knock me down and knock me down again. Finally, I come up against the fence and I thought surely he was abouts to kill me dead. I pulled up a fence post with my good hand and whopped him one right in the head." The aged black sheep closed his eyes, remembering the blow.

"It was one mighty clobberin'," he said, his voice lower than before. "And it was Daddy, not me, that come out of it dead." His voice faded to a weak, hoarse whisper. "I dragged a bunch of logs over and piled 'em right on top his body. Then I set it all to fire."

The black sheep then cried out in fright, thinking that his father was in the room, standing behind the gathered men. He died pointing his finger in the air, frozen in place, pointing to an empty spot just inside the door.

The brothers noticed a man's face on the side of Rumbling Bald when they returned home for the burial, but they suspected that if they'd looked closer they might have seen it when the search for their missing father began. They speculated that the face on the rock had been caused by the smoke rising from their father's burning body. There was no mistaking the features, they agreed. It was their father who looked down on them from the mountain.

The battling brothers may have given the mountain its face, but it was the earthquake of 1874 and its aftereffects that gave Rumbling Bald its name. From January to early summer of that year, the mountain was lifted into prominence, its eastern edge quaking into existence with loud, thunderous rolls that shook the valley below. Tremors startled residents of Rutherfordton seventeen miles to the east and vibrated window glass into dust.

The alarming shocks during the six months of initial activity caused great distress among the inhabitants of the immediate area. Many who believed that they were witnessing the birth of a volcano fled the area in fear of lava spills. Superstitious mountain folk believed it was the devil himself rising from the pits of hell to claim the souls of the sinful. One area church was said to have accepted twenty-five new memberships among those who chose to stay.

The noises continued. They were, in fact, the sounds of huge boulders dislodged by the opening of a deep crack in the side of the mountain. Smoke was said to rise from the gaping fissure whenever the strange rumbling noises were heard in the valley below—even long after the summer of 1874. For nearly seventy years, each resounding internal boom of the mountain was cause for renewed alarm among restless inhabitants.

Members of the National Speleological Society traveled from Washington, D.C., in the summer of 1940 in an attempt to explain the noises and the trails of smoke that issued from Rumbling Bald once and for all. They explored the fissure and its surrounding area. Too deep to be measured, the crack was seven feet wide at some points and was still expanding each year along its half-mile length. The fissure's continued growth accounted for the internal rumblings of the mountain. Boulders lodged inside the fissure fell as the crack widened.

The scientists clambered inside the fissure at different points, entering far enough to document a honeycombed system of deep caverns. The shapes of several of these caves allowed them to act as echo chambers, their steep sides sounding boards for boulders that tumbled down the fissure to the bottoms of the caverns.

What about the smoke? The team of investigators suggested that the smoke rising from the fissure was merely dust lifting from the activity of the rocks. Some smoke, they added, might be the result of shale decomposition.

When they looked at the face on Rumbling Bald, others preferred to believe that the rumblings and quakes were the effects of a feud among giant men in the woods. The smoke was left over from the burning of a father's fallen body. And the face, the face itself, looking back at you in silence, seemed to know the secret of why it was there.

THE MAGIC THAT
BROUGHT BACK TOBACCO
••••••••••••
••

Perhaps no plant other than the tree of knowledge in the Garden of Eden has so influenced the destinies of countless men and women as has the broad, dried leaf of tobacco.

Tobacco was indigenous to North America, but the type that is grown commercially was originally imported from the West Indies. Burley, a popular cigarette tobacco, grew well in the sandy soil of the North Carolina mountains and was the leading cash crop in the region for years. Tobacco was grown commercially in every county of western North Carolina, and the fortunes of the industry accounted for much of the state's financial progress following the War Between the States.

Matthew Micksch opened a tobacco shop in Winston-Salem as long ago as 1773. More than a hundred years later, R. J. Reynolds built his first tobacco factory in 1875. James B. "Buck" Duke died in 1925, leaving behind an $80 million endowment for Durham-area hospitals and for Duke University in particular. Buck Duke's fortune was based upon the manufacture of cigarettes and the development of the Bull Durham blend of smoking tobacco. In organizing the American Tobacco Company of Durham, North Carolina, Buck Duke did for tobacco what Rockefeller did for oil and Carnegie did for steel.

Long before Christopher Columbus returned to the court of Queen Isabella with samples of tobacco, however, the inhabitants of western North Carolina had incorporated the smoking of the dried plant into their celebrations and religious ceremonies. Tobacco, called tso-lungh in Cherokee, was considered sacred because of its medical and magical powers.

In the beginning of the world, according to Cherokee legend, people and animals conversed. Many animals at this time were, in fact, people in slightly different form. There was only one tobacco plant, and people enjoyed picking one of its broad leaves and smoking it in their pipes from time to time.

Dagul-Ku is the Cherokee name for a goose believed by some to be the American white-fronted goose. The goose was very rare in the mountains of western North Carolina. Its bluish white coat of feathers resembled the color of tobacco smoke. One day, Dagul-Ku decided to take the tobacco plant for himself and the other geese who lived to the east.

The magical powers of tobacco smoke were so strong and the people missed it so severely that many took sick. It was feared that some of the elderly Cherokee might die for want of tobacco smoke. A young warrior volunteered to make his way to the place where Dagul-Ku was keeping the plant and return with it.

It was a dangerous mission through the evil pass known today as Hickory Nut Gap, which was ruled by a malicious tribe of diminutive spirits. The small ghost people who populated the cliffs and caverns were rarely seen. They were known to hate the Cherokee enough to throw boulders upon any Indian who attempted to walk through the gap. The most dangerous part of the gap was at the current-day town of Chimney Rock, North

Carolina, situated in a deep valley beneath the rock formation of the same name. The gap narrows to a mere trail along the Rocky Broad River. At this point, the river curves sharply among large, jagged rocks.

A Cherokee needed a great deal of magic on his side to walk through the pass at Hickory Nut Gap. A few days after the young warrior had left, a small bird flew into the village to tell the people that the warrior had not survived the attack of the little spirits. He was killed when the small, evil ghosts threw a boulder upon him at the place where the gap narrowed.

In an effort to save an old woman who had grown quite frail and thin without tobacco, the Cherokee asked the animals to help. Since the little spirits did not hate animals as badly as they did people, many animals made it safely through the gap. But Dagul-Ku proved to be a vigilant guard of the tobacco plant. The biting goose ran off one animal after another as they approached the plant. Finally, the mole volunteered to go, believing he could burrow underground and avoid Dagul-Ku and the other geese. The geese, however, saw the small hump the mole created as he burrowed toward the plant. They set upon the ground in a rage, forced the mole to come up for air, and killed him.

By then it was clear that the elderly woman was about to die. Many others had grown ill, and tobacco was desperately needed to save them. At the moment of deepest despair and frustration, a very old man of the village came out of his house on his cane and told the others that he could bring tobacco back from the place where Dagul-Ku had hidden it. No one believed him at first. But the elderly one had been singing his prayers every day since the goose had stolen their plant, and he claimed he was now ready to perform this awesome task for his people.

The old man was known to be of good character and in close touch with the world of the spirits. Because the toothless old man also possessed a laugh that sounded like the cackle and honking of geese flying overhead, it was agreed that he might succeed. A man who could laugh like a goose could perhaps defeat Dagul-Ku.

In his prayers, the old magician had asked the hummingbird how he flew so swiftly, and the secret had been revealed to him. He traveled from the Cherokee village to Hickory Nut Gap, where he fasted and concentrated on his songs. The next day, he removed from his medicine bag a small bundle of colorful hummingbird feathers. The old man sang a powerful song and rubbed his body with the feathers until he turned into a hummingbird.

Moving through the sky toward the sun, the old magician flew swiftly through the gap along the river. The old man was so small and flew so swiftly that he was not noticed by the evil spirits who inhabited the crags and rocks overlooking the gorge. Flying frontwards and backwards, sideways and up and down in rapid, spinning motions, he made his way safely by Dagul-Ku. The hummingbird snatched away as much of the tobacco plant as he could carry and flew swiftly back, little more than a blur in the sky. His return to the village was greeted with much singing.

While he was gone, the old woman had died. Her body lay in her house, where she was surrounded by mourners. Other people in the village had taken a turn for the worse and were very near death. The old man transformed himself quickly from a hummingbird to his natural shape. He crumbled some of the fragrant tobacco leaf into his clay pipe and lit it. Then the old man deeply inhaled the blue smoke and blew it gently into the nostrils of the old woman everyone believed to be dead. To the surprise of the mourners, the smoke revived the frail woman, and she sat up and soon regained her strength.

The elderly Cherokee magician treated all the others in the same manner, and they also responded well.

By the time that everyone in the village breathed the healing smoke from the leaf brought back by the hummingbird, the tobacco had run out. Once again, the people were faced with the illness and death sure to befall them if more tobacco was not rescued from Dagul-Ku.

A council was held and this time the men of the village immediately sought the old man's assistance. They entered his house with words of praise and asked the magician what he might do now to retrieve the plant for their people. It was pointed out that a hummingbird could never carry back enough tobacco for the Cherokee to remain healthy for long.

Being a hummingbird had taught the old man many mysteries of the world. He devised a way to increase his power so that he might retrieve the entire tobacco plant from Dagul-Ku's guard. When he told the council this, they asked that on his journey he also look for the body of the young warrior who had been sent on the first quest. The old magician promised to do this and asked to be left alone for several days.

He prayed and fasted for four days, then left the village. He spent a night in the woods without going to sleep. There he asked the advice of the birds and they told him what to do to increase his magic. By morning, the old magician was ready.

This time, he turned himself into a huge hummingbird instead of one of normal size. Again, he flew toward the sun as he approached Hickory Nut Gap. This time, the furious beating of his wings created a circular wind so strong that it stripped the cliffs of all vegetation and brought down many rocks from the steep rise of the mountains.

As he flew, it appeared as if a roaring whirlwind moved through the gorge. The wind was a virtual tornado, so loud and destructive that it frightened the evil spirits of the cliffs. They hid inside their caves and fissures and have never been seen since except as small, harmless ghosts that occasionally appear near Chimney Rock.

Dagul-Ku and the other geese flew away in terror, honking

loudly as they made their way north to the places they lived in spring and summer. The old magician was tired by his flight and a little frightened of the power of his own magic. He picked up the entire tobacco plant with ease and flew back to Hickory Nut Gap. As he approached the gorge, he grew completely weary and changed back into an old man.

It was a long walk home, but he could now pass safely through the gap. Walking by Chimney Rock, following the course of the river, the old man was troubled by the destruction his whirlwind flight had caused, even though his magic had been for his people's good. He realized the land would never be the same.

Carrying the sack that contained the shells, stones, and feathers necessary for his magic, the elderly Cherokee with the toothless laugh diligently searched among the fallen rocks littering the narrow valley for the body of the young warrior who had been the first to try to rescue the tobacco plant from Dagul-Ku.

The tired old man finally located the bones of the young Cherokee in the river. The aged magician used the last of his powers to bring the young warrior back to life. Then the two set out to return to their village. The younger man carried the sack. He also cut a walking stick from the undergrowth for the old man. They made slow progress, the magician laboring over the rocks on the twisting floor of the gorge.

The young warrior's purity had to be proven before he could be allowed to carry the sacred tobacco plant back to his people. They came upon a large tree with a thick trunk. There was a hole in the trunk resembling a window or door at the height of its lowest branches. A very lovely woman looked out upon the two men from the window in the tree. It seemed to the young man that she was beckoning him to join her in her home inside the tree.

The young warrior asked the old man to guard the tobacco sack. Then he climbed the tree to reach the woman.

But the Cherokee discovered that no matter how hard he attempted to clamber up the trunk, the first branches remained out of reach. The beautiful woman continued to smile down at him. The warrior dropped to the ground and asked the old magician to help. The old man brought out from his medicine sack a special pair of moccasins. After putting them on, the young warrior found he could easily climb the tree.

Though he scrambled as quickly as he could, the hole and the maiden remained out of reach. It was as if the tree grew toward the sky as rapidly as he climbed, both rising higher and higher at the same rate. Without counsel from the old magician, the young man finally abandoned his quest for the beautiful woman.

The warrior had to pass through many layers of clouds as he climbed back down. Only upon reaching the ground did the young Cherokee realize that the appearance of the beckoning maiden had been a test of his true spirit. By refusing to climb the tree any further, he proved his commitment to returning to earth and finishing the journey to the village with the elderly magician.

The two were welcomed with many shouts. Dances were held in their honor. The tobacco was replanted and its leaves carefully harvested. When the proper time came, seeds from the tobacco Dagul-Ku had stolen were also planted, and soon there was tobacco in abundance among the Cherokee of western North Carolina.

GHOSTS AND GOLD
IN A WORLD OF WATER AND STONE
·············
··

Long a place where spirits appeared to the early Cherokee people, Chimney Rock Mountain was the site of a British mining party's lost fortune and two of the most dramatic and well-documented appearances of ghosts in all of North America. A more fitting natural landscape for visitations from the spirit world cannot be found.

A twenty-five-hundred-foot monolith of granite and greenery, Chimney Rock Mountain helps to form the southern boundary at the eastern gateway into Hickory Nut Gap. The town of Chimney Rock stands at the mountain's base in a portion of the gap so deep and narrow that it forms a gorge. The granite mountain rises above the Rocky Broad River, appearing as a towering cliff when viewed from the river below.

A large portion of the rocky bluff hangs out over the gorge. Midway up the front of the mountain stands an isolated pillar of rock, a circular stone rising 225 feet from the mountain itself. It is this tower of granite for which the mountain and the town are named.

Near the summit is a rock in the shape of a human head, known locally as Devil's Head, that keeps an eerie watch over the valley below. Nearby, Hickory Nut Falls plummets four hundred feet over another portion of the magnificent cliff.

The gorge is a wild world of water and of stone, the Rocky Broad River twisting and curving around large, broken rocks of granite that fill its bed. At the base of the stone mountains, waterfalls have formed three deep, circular pools near Lake Lure. The cascading water has carved three symmetrical pools in a floor of smooth granite over the centuries. The Bottomless Pools are one of the valley's true scenic wonders. These geological formations are among the oldest known in the world.

Long ago, precious minerals including gold were mined in the Blue Ridge Mountains of North Carolina. Round Top, the mountain opposite Chimney Rock and a little to the north, forms the other wall of the steep gorge between. A treasure of mined gold is believed to have been hidden there.

In the 1700s, a small group of Englishmen owned and operated a gold mine just north of Round Top. They planned to journey to the Atlantic coast with a year's worth of gold, then on to England, where they would marry the girls who patiently awaited their return.

Traveling through Hickory Nut Gap on horseback with mules carrying their treasure of gold, the Englishmen were surprised by a body of Indians. Fearing the Cherokee hunters knew what they transported, the Englishmen fired upon the group to frighten them away, and a battle ensued. As warriors from surrounding Cherokee camps joined the fracas, the Englishmen were forced to retreat.

The miners found shelter in a cave. All but one of the Englishmen were killed. The lone survivor escaped into the night on foot after erecting a wall of stones across the mouth of the cave. He made his way to the coast and set sail for England, where he organized a party to return for the gold.

As fate would have it, the fellow went blind before he could book passage back to the colonies. However, he dictated a map that showed where the gold was hidden and financed a search party. The small group was dispatched to the North Carolina mountains to locate the cave and return with the gold. But they returned empty-handed.

Word of the gold hidden in a secret cave spread far and wide. Since that time, numerous groups and individuals have scoured the mountains in an attempt to locate the missing fortune. One of the most persistent treasure hunters proved to be General Collett Leventhorpe of Rutherfordton, one of North Carolina's few generals in the Confederate army. General Leventhorpe brought a group of about fifty men to Round Top Mountain and spent two months searching for the cave. The search grew too costly, and General Leventhorpe ultimately abandoned the hunt without result.

In September of 1938, the *Forest City Courier* carried an account of a latter-day treasure hunter who came to Round Top Mountain with a map that appeared to provide detailed directions to the Englishman's cave. After an extensive search of the area, the venture proved unsuccessful. Apparently, the forces of nature had so changed the mountain that no map was of much help. It was concluded that the mouth of the cave had been covered by a rock slide.

If anyone has found the gold, it has yet to be reported. Rumors of a map continue to circulate. Occasionally, the Library of Congress has even received requests for a manuscript that shows the location of a cave near Chimney Rock, North Carolina, where gold was said to have been hidden by a party of eighteenth-century Englishmen. However, the Library of Congress has never been able to locate such a map.

It isn't strange that this spectacular world of water and stone, of high cliffs, cascading water, and secret caverns, has long been an area of mythic quality in the mountains of western North Carolina. Hickory Nut Gorge and Chimney Rock Mountain itself are also a world of spirits and ghosts.

For generations, the Cherokee spoke of a multitude of small, evil spirits inhabiting the vicinity of Hickory Nut Gorge and Chimney Rock Mountain, but it took a couple of well-documented nineteenth-century sightings to raise the local lore to prominence.

The appearance of a ghostly horde on July 31, 1806, was widely published in newspapers of the time. On that summer evening, eight-year-old Elizabeth Reaves looked up from her play to see the apparition of a pale man standing on Chimney Rock. Patsey Reaves, a widow, believed her daughter was simply manufacturing a childhood fantasy. But the little girl was persistent, insisting that she'd not only seen the man rolling bright white rocks down the side of the mountain and waving sticks, but that she'd also seen "a heap of people." The widow and her children lived within a mile of Chimney Rock Mountain.

Morgan Reaves, Elizabeth's eleven-year-old brother, added that he'd seen something as well. According to an account in the September 15, 1806, edition of the *Raleigh Register*, Morgan told his mother that he'd seen "a thousand or ten thousand things flying in the air" above Chimney Rock.

Accompanied by her fourteen-year-old daughter, Polly, the widow approached the place where the younger children had been playing, in an effort to humor them and to calm their excitement. As the evening breeze swept gently through the gorge, Patsey Reaves shaded her eyes with her hand and looked up at Chimney Rock. She was startled by what she saw. Along the upper ridge, Patsey viewed "a very numerous crowd of beings resembling the human species," as the *Raleigh Register* reported. "They were of every size, from the tallest of men down to the least infants," Patsey said. "And they were all clad in white raiment."

The ghosts appeared to be flying or walking on the air around Chimney Rock. "When all but a few had reached the rock, two seemed to rise together, and behind them a third rose," Patsey claimed. "These three then moved with great agility towards the crowd and had the nearest resemblance to men of any seen before."

According to published accounts, the ghostly spectacle continued for more than an hour. The awestruck Patsey Reaves eventually sent for a neighbor, a man named Robert Siercy. When he arrived, the enthralling activities of the white, glowing ghosts were far from over.

Siercy reported that he saw "more glittering white appearances of humankind than ever I had seen of men" gathered in one place. "They moved in throngs around the large rock, and so passed along in a southern course between me and the mountain to the place where Patsey said they rose." Siercy said that two spirits of "full size went before the general crowd," leading them back to the place from which they'd risen. There, the spirits vanished from sight.

The children and adults who witnessed the ritual dance of the floating ghosts upon Chimney Rock were not terrified by the spectacle. Indeed, Siercy reported that when the ghosts vanished he was left with "a solemn and pleasing impression on the mind," although this was accompanied by a weakness of physical strength.

No one has successfully explained Chimney Rock's ghosts. Many have argued that the sighting was a mirage. George Newton, an area reverend who interviewed Patsey Reaves and Robert Siercy, published an account that suggested the dance of the spirits might have been "a prelude to the descent of the Holy City."

The sighting by Reaves and Siercy would easily qualify Chimney Rock Mountain as a place of mystery, if not of magic. Yet a short five years later, in 1811, another unearthly spectacle complete with sound effects took place on Chimney Rock.

Silas McDowell of Rutherfordton visited the area to interview those who witnessed the 1811 apparition, and it is McDowell's transcript that survives today, edited by Gary S. Dunbar and published in the December 1961 issue of the *North Carolina Folklore Journal*.

The witnesses to the latter visit of ghostly spirits to Chimney Rock were an old man and his wife who lived in the valley below. The retelling of what the old couple saw created so much excitement in the area that a public meeting was held in nearby Rutherfordton. A delegation including a magistrate and a clerk was sent to visit the old couple. Accounts were published in local newspapers.

Silas McDowell and his contemporaries knew Hickory Nut Gorge as Chimney Rock Pass. The old man and his wife had been seated in their yard "in the deepest portion of Chimney Rock Pass," McDowell wrote, at the time of evening when shadows had taken over the narrow valley but sunlight still illuminated the summits of the mountains.

"Their attention was arrested by the astounding spectacle," McDowell continued, of "two opposing armies of horsemen, high up in the air, all mounted on winged horses and preparing for combat."

At length, the cry of "Charge!" was heard, and the two ghost cavalries "dashed at each other," according to McDowell's account, "cutting, thrusting, and hacking." The ring of their clashing swords was clearly heard, and the couple saw the glint of sunlight flash from the uplifted blades. "They fought for about ten minutes, when one army was routed and left the field. The shouts of the victors and the wails of the defeated were heard plainly, soon after which darkness hid both armies from view."

McDowell reported that on subsequent evenings the ghosts of mounted cavalrymen were seen, "but not in battle." He further claimed that he'd located three respectable men who had witnessed the same phenomenon from their houses in the valley below Chimney Rock.

What he had reported haunted McDowell throughout his life. He was not a man to believe in ghosts. Many years later, he offered what he considered the definitive explanation of what the elderly couple and the three men had seen. "In autumn, when the atmosphere is clear before a change in the weather, the lower atmosphere of the ravine is charged with vapor," he wrote. "Seen through this medium, the vapor acts with telescopic effect and swells in size a bunch of gnats at play in the sun's rays to the appearance of a squadron of winged horses."

McDowell further suggested that the flashing swords were the magnified glimmer of the gnats' wings and that the clashing of swords heard so clearly by the witnesses was actually the echo of cowbells.

Many disagree with this assessment. The two documented accounts of ghosts over Chimney Rock lead even skeptical minds to consider the possibility that something supernatural may have occurred. Whether they accept Silas McDowell's theory of the gnats or not, visitors to Hickory Nut Gap will find it difficult to take issue with McDowell's description of the gorge. "Chimney Rock Pass is one of Nature's sublimest poems," he wrote, "where objects are so weird, beautiful, and grand that words cannot translate them, and they can only be seen and felt when we look, wonder, and admire in dumb amazement."

HANNIBAL HEATON
HEARS A HOOT

Geneneral Wade Hampton was still alive when Mrs. Heaton, who loved the place she lived more than any other place in the world, changed herself into an owl.

Confederate General Wade Hampton, governor of South Carolina from 1876 to 1879 and later a United States senator, built High Hampton Inn in 1850 on his twenty-two-hundred-acre estate just southeast of Cashiers in Jackson County. Known as the "Giant in Gray," General Hampton spent his summers at High Hampton until his death in 1902.

General Hampton's nephew was Dr. William S. Halstead, chief of surgery at Johns Hopkins in Baltimore. In the 1890s, Dr. Halstead was looking for some land for a summer estate and retirement home. He decided on a green tract near High Hampton Inn known as Heaton Field, and he promptly made an offer of sixteen hundred dollars to the owners, Hannibal Heaton and his wife, Loesa Emmalie.

The Heatons were a highly recognizable couple. Hannibal was short and sported a long, red mustache that entirely covered his mouth. Loesa was pretty, though not frail. It was said her hair turned white while she was still in her twenties because it looked good that way.

The Heatons had always been known as a happy couple, but the prospect of selling their land to Dr. Halstead threatened to break up their marriage. Hannibal wanted to sell. Mrs. Heaton didn't. Hannibal found convincing her to go along with the deal was more difficult than herding a train of elephants over the Alps. Mrs. Heaton insisted that there was no other place in the world she wanted to live.

Some people make a different resolution every year. Others make the same resolution year after year and never keep it. Mrs. Heaton resolved to stay on their land near High Hampton, and she meant it. In fact, she told Hannibal that if he sold the land, she wouldn't leave. She said she'd just hang herself from the tree out front, and that would be that.

Dr. Halstead never imagined the trouble he caused. Hannibal Heaton didn't believe his wife meant what she said. He thought she was only being stubborn and that sooner or later things would get back to normal. Hannibal had the deed drawn up in Dr. Halstead's name and turned it over to him.

But word of the transaction got home before Hannibal did. Driving his wagon into the yard that evening, long after it had grown dark, he saw a ghostly female figure swinging from a rope tied to a branch of the tree in the front yard—it turned out to be Loesa. Mrs. Heaton had hung herself just as she'd promised.

Hannibal should have listened. With a sorrowful heart, he climbed the tree intending to cut down his wife's body, but something kept him from it. Perched directly above Mrs. Heaton's body on the branch the rope was tied to was a huge, white owl. The night bird screeched at Hannibal as he reached out to cut the rope, forcing him to withdraw.

The owl refused to budge. It proved so stubborn that Hannibal went inside to get his shotgun. Taking aim at the large bird easily visible even in the darkness, Hannibal found that he could not squeeze the trigger. The bird was the same color as his wife's striking hair. And there was something in its eyes that reminded him of Loesa.

The white owl had upset him so, Hannibal Heaton had to drive his wagon to the neighbors to get their help in removing his wife from the tree. It was said that his mustache turned a light gray that night. From then on, Hannibal always fidgeted with his hands, chewed his mustache constantly, and was unable to focus his eyes in one direction for more than a second or two. All agreed that the nervous condition was brought on by the death of his wife.

Yet Hannibal didn't believe his wife had died. He insisted that the white owl that refused to leave the tree in the front yard was Loesa. Nothing could convince him otherwise. The owl sat on its branch outside his window every night, and its haunting "hoo-hoo-hoot" filled the house.

Mrs. Heaton was buried in nearby Zachary Cemetery. On her tombstone was inscribed, "She was ready to every good work."

Hannibal could have remained in the house until the following summer, when Dr. Halstead had agreed to take possession of the property, but the widower Heaton disappeared within a week of his wife's burial. No one ever heard of Hannibal Heaton again. But the people in High Hampton still hear from Mrs. Heaton.

The original High Hampton Inn was destroyed by fire in 1932 and was rebuilt later that same year. High Hampton is now a resort that provides refuge for owls, especially one large, white owl with bright, blinking eyes. It's said that this white owl can sometimes be seen in the evening near the inn as it hunts from perches among the trees and shrubbery.

And when the white owl can't be seen, it can be heard giving a hoot that carries across Hampton Lake, across Heaton Field, and all the way to Whiteside Mountain, a hoot that sounds more like a human's cry than that of a bird of prey. Old-timers are likely to tell you it's old Mrs. Heaton.

Who knows? Maybe owls are more stubborn than mules, and maybe Loesa Heaton never left her land after all.

THE WICKED WITCH
OF NANTAHALA
••••••••••••
••

In days long past, there were more than snarling bears and mountain panthers to frighten children in the hills of western North Carolina. There was Spearfinger, a woman-monster who fed on human livers.

Spearfinger, a singularly nasty witch known to the Cherokee, feasted on unsuspecting children throughout the mountains. She was, however, particularly associated with Whiteside Mountain, a prominent peak at an elevation of 4,950 feet, one side of which is a highly visible 1,800-foot sheer cliff. This solid rock face is the highest exposed-rock cliff in the eastern United States.

In this part of the Nantahala National Forest just off U.S. Highway 64 between Cashiers and Highlands, the mountain woods are thick with towering hemlocks and spruce.

Banks of the stream near Whiteside are quilted with moss and crisscrossed with the delicate lace of thriving ferns. But it's the rocks that contribute most to the visual drama of Whiteside Mountain.

The area is littered with rocks. A jutting formation on the east side of Whiteside Mountain is known locally as the Devil's Courthouse, while a particularly large boulder about halfway up the same outcropping of rocks is claimed to be Satan's throne.

It was from these very rocks that the witch Spearfinger sprang. A terrifying witch, Spearfinger possessed the power to take on any appearance she chose, including that of the rocks. In her true form, Spearfinger looked something like an old woman, with some notable differences.

The ancient witch, who outlived generation upon generation of man, was yellowish in appearance. Her entire body was covered by a hard skin of rock, a skin so dense it proved impenetrable by arrow or ax. Spearfinger could best be identified by the form of her right hand, one finger of which was long and pointed, resembling an awl. The witch used her finger to fatally stab anyone unlucky enough to come within the range of her sharpened reach.

In her true form, the vicious witch also possessed a strong, horrible smell, which she could at times mask when people came near. Yet her natural malodorous state was so severe that Spearfinger was crawling with flies. Among the Cherokee, it was known that the hum of flies in the mountain forest meant that Spearfinger might be hiding somewhere nearby.

When hungry, Spearfinger altered her appearance to that of a sweet old lady, the flies vanishing, her stone skin disguised. The evil witch had enormous powers over stone and could easily move huge rocks. She could cement two stones together simply by striking one against the other. And she could turn herself into stone to keep from being found in the rocky terrain of the mountains.

To travel through the rugged country more easily, Spearfinger set about building a great bridge between Whiteside Mountain and a distant peak. The bridge was well under way when it was struck by lightning. The fragments of Spearfinger's stone bridge were scattered at the base of Whiteside Mountain. Pieces of her bridge are still visible today throughout the region.

Spearfinger favored hiding at the heads of mountain streams and in the dark passes and hollows of the Nantahala Gorge, where other Indian evils were known to lurk. She ventured throughout the area in search of her favorite food, however, and anyone who came across her in the mountains was a likely victim of her ferocious appetite for human livers. Spearfinger was especially fond of children.

At the time of Spearfinger, the rich bottomlands of the Nantahala National Forest were noted for their abundance of strawberries and other wild fruits and berries. Cherokee children were often sent into the hollows and grassy areas along the rushing streams to pick wild strawberries for their village. The children were especially vulnerable at these times. Many were snatched away by Spearfinger.

At other times, when no child could be found at the wooded edges of the rocky mountain forests, Spearfinger would venture closer to the villages, watching with hungry eyes from behind a tattered shawl for any child she might be able to seize.

Spearfinger would call to the children, referring to them as her grandchildren. There is no word for grandchild in the Cherokee language. Cherokee endearingly addressed their grandchildren as "my son's children" or "children of my daughter." The endearment was particularly alluring when spoken by a kind old lady with gray hair who hid her smile behind a shawl.

"Come," Spearfinger would call. "Come, my little girl, and let your grandmother dress your hair."

The witch hid her mouth because her teeth were made of sharp, broken pieces of stone that would scare the children away.

She was also careful to keep her awl finger hidden beneath her shawl. When one of the girls ambled over, the wicked witch laid the child's head in her lap. She petted and combed the child's hair with the fingers of her other hand until the little darling fell fast asleep.

Then, with her rock-and-bone finger, the hungry witch stabbed the napping child through the heart. Spearfinger quickly removed the child's liver with her blood-smeared awl finger and ate it on the spot. As the old witch chewed, she gradually returned to her true form, her skin hardening and taking on its yellow cast, the fetid smell rising as flies came to light upon her wretched, laughing face.

Warriors would follow the trail of buzzing flies and drying blood into the dense forest, but with no result. Spearfinger simply changed herself into a pile of rocks or a single boulder whenever anyone came after her. After the murder of village children, she was occasionally discovered in the form of stone by Cherokee warriors when a particular boulder or human-sized pile of stones was covered with flies. But the warriors could do little to harm the witch. Many arrows and spears were broken in an attempt to kill Spearfinger after she'd changed herself into a rock. Should the warrior touch the rock, he'd be tainted with the smell of the witch as if he'd been sprayed by a skunk, and he would have to sleep outside his home for at least four days before he was permitted to enter again. The unlucky Cherokee spent those four days fighting off flies.

Cherokee children were particularly vulnerable to attack in autumn. This was the time of leaf burning, when the Cherokee burned fallen leaves from the forest floor before shaking chestnuts from the trees. The old witch was always on the lookout for trails of smoke among the trees of the Nantahala Forest in autumn. She knew that the children of the villages would be gathering the nuts and wandering to the edges of the mountainside. The wrinkled crone would patiently wait, sharpening her appetite, waiting to change into a gentle old grandmother and surprise a hapless child who was accidentally separated from the others. Cherokee elders, the actual grandparents of the children, tried diligently to keep the children together as they gathered chestnuts.

The witch of Whiteside Mountain became a pronounced danger when she could find no children in the forests on whom to dine. She ventured progressively closer to the villages, watching with hungry eyes from behind her tattered shawl for any child she might be able to seize. Spearfinger might ultimately summon her powers and enter a village in search of a meal. She'd wait until she spied a family member leaving a house. Instantly, the hungry witch took on the appearance of the family member and entered the home. So swift was Spearfinger and so sharp her finger that at these times she could stab a child without the victim's even knowing it. The witch left no wound and caused no pain, quickly removing the liver and carrying it off into the night, where she could eat it in safety while slowly changing back to her yellowed form. The child who was her victim went about his affairs until all at once he felt weak and grew ill. Eventually, the child pined away and died because Spearfinger had stolen from his small body its tender liver.

On rare occasions a solitary hunter spotted Spearfinger walking in the forest. Her hand was visible even from a distance, appearing at first glance as if she were carrying a knife. No hunter came too near because the strong odor of Spearfinger warned him off.

The witch was said to sing along with the hum of the flies that accompanied her as she walked among the rocks and trees, climbing carefully up the mountainside. It was rather a pretty song, sung in a low voice like a lullaby, but one that told of the many sweet livers of children Spearfinger had consumed. More than one hunter lifted his bow and arrow, his blood chilled by the words of the witch's song, and took aim at the dreadful creature, only to watch his arrow bounce off her hardened skin or break in two upon contact. The hunter would then hurry away in silent fright back to his village to tell his story of Spearfinger.

So many children died in the area of Whiteside Mountain that the Cherokee called a great council to devise a manner to rid the forest of the wicked she-monster before everyone was killed. Indians traveled from many villages to attend the council. After much debate, it was decided that the best way to kill Spearfinger was to trap her in a pitfall. Then all the warriors could attack her at once.

The pitfall was known among nearly all the Indians of the eastern United States, but was used only to catch especially large or dangerous game. A pit was dug along a trail and covered with underbrush. The animal was chased along the trail until it stumbled upon the pitfall and fell snarling into the deep trap.

The Cherokee dug a pit across the trail outside their village and covered it with leaves, twigs, and small, brittle branches. They were careful to line the trail with similar autumn leaves so that Spearfinger would not discern that the ground had been disturbed. To entice the witch, the Indians lit a fire on the other side of the trail before hiding themselves in the shrubbery.

Spearfinger saw the trail of smoke and smacked her lips. She believed the children had been sent out from the village to gather chestnuts. The witch made her way down Whiteside Mountain.

The hidden warriors waited. Eventually, an old woman wearing a shawl came along the trail. Several of the young men wanted to shoot her upon sight, but the closer she came the more it appeared that this old woman with gray hair might not be the wicked witch they meant to kill. In fact, she looked exactly like an old woman of the village they all knew well.

After some hushed debate, the warriors let the woman pass unmolested. If she were the woman from the village, she would know they'd built a pitfall, they reasoned. The Indians had already pointed out to each other that this elderly woman kept her right hand covered by her shawl.

With a loud crash, Spearfinger tumbled into the pitfall. Upon landing at the bottom of the deep hole, she changed instantly into her true, yellow form. A swarm of late-season flies followed her into the pit. No longer a feeble old woman, the stony-skinned Spearfinger snarled and raged in a rasping, terrible voice as the warriors encircled the pit, weapons poised. She ranted curses upon the Cherokee around the sharp, broken rocks that were her teeth. The odor of the witch was so strong that many of the warriors had to back away from the rim of the pit after firing an arrow at the yellow witch.

The battle had just begun. The savage liver-eater scrambled up one side of the pit, then the other, reaching out with her bone finger in all directions, looking for someone to stab. The warriors beat Spearfinger back by throwing large rocks, but they did no damage other than to cause the woman-monster to fall back down into the hole.

The warriors grew frantic. Though they fired their arrows straight and true and as rapidly as they were able, the weapons proved useless against Spearfinger's stony skin. The arrows broke and fell like snapped twigs all around the witch.

Spearfinger taunted the men, certain she would eventually climb out of the pit and get at them. A small bird the Cherokee call tsi-kilili, the Carolina chickadee, watched from a nearby spruce branch and began to sing to the warriors. The Cherokee know the chickadee as a truth teller. The bird swooped into the pit, singing, "Here, here, here." The chickadee bravely alighted on the yellow witch's deadly finger, and try as she might Spearfinger could not shake it loose. The warriors understood that tsi-kilili was instructing them to fire their arrows at her right hand. They did so, and as an arrow struck the witch's palm she let out a piercing scream. Her wounded hand poured forth a great quantity of blood.

The chickadee lifted in flight as the old witch withered and died.

Many demons and witches of the mountains were known to hide their hearts in secret places so they couldn't be killed. Spearfinger always kept her right hand clenched because she carried her heart in her hand. Tsi-kilili had somehow learned Spearfinger's secret, and the small bird remains a welcome friend among the Cherokee.

The witch was buried where she lay, at the bottom of the pit. Some believe Spearfinger turned herself into one of the rocks in the pitfall and lived to stalk today.

It is still considered a foreboding of bad luck when a fly is found buzzing around a rock in the Nantahala National Forest in autumn. Cherokee hunters will change direction to keep from hiking beyond such a spot. The warning is considered especially severe if the fly is seen in November, long after the killing October frosts have turned the leaves.

X MARKS THE SPOT
•••••••••••••
••

One cold night in January of 1875, two adventurous men sat inside a home in Hutchinson, Kansas, and talked about their dream of building a brand-new town in what would be the most perfect spot in America. Samuel T. Kelsey and Charles Hutchinson bent over a map spread out upon a table. Outside, a frozen rain was carried on the prairie wind.

Kelsey patiently explained his theory of locating the prime spot upon which to build the town. To demonstrate to Hutchinson, he brought out a ruler and a pencil and drew two heavy lines upon the map of the United States. One line was drawn between Chicago and Savannah. A second connected New Orleans and Baltimore. The two lines formed an X.

"We'll build the town where the lines cross," Kelsey said. "It's the perfect place."

The X marked a spot near where the states of North Carolina, South Carolina, and Georgia converge. Kelsey convinced his partner that the intersection of the two lines would become the exact center of population of the eastern United States. It was his firm belief that people would come through the town in droves to reach every point in that part of the country.

The flatlanders had been eyeing the prairie too long. Their theory might have made sense as the crow flies, assuming the land at the intersection of their two lines was as flat as Kansas. What they didn't realize was that in the western part of North Carolina that is now the Nantahala National Forest, even crows opt to fly around the summits instead of over them.

Leaving their families and homes, Kelsey and Hutchinson made their way to Atlanta that same January and headed northwest by mule into the rugged hill country. They wandered in the mountains for days, finally climbing out of Georgia to locate the lofty plateau on Satulah Mountain that they christened Highlands, North Carolina.

They had some thinking to do. The 3,835-foot peak was a rough place to attempt to build a town. Faced with the sheer ruggedness of the region and the fact that there were no existing roads, Kelsey and Hutchinson merely shrugged their shoulders and refused to waver from their dream. They purchased eight hundred acres of the western plateau of the mountain, land from which they could look down into Georgia.

They had the area surveyed, then cut an east–west road straight through the center of the acreage. Hutchinson took for himself a forty-two-acre tract on the south side of "Main Street," while Kelsey claimed a similar tract on the north side. Kelsey and Hutchinson were the only citizens of their town.

As a matter of luck, the men had chosen one of the most biologically significant spots in North Carolina. The variety of local plant and animal life is a virtual encyclopedia of the southeastern mountains, since the plateau is a transitional area between climatic zones. The forests boast the rare *Shortia*—an evergreen with nodding, bell-shaped, white flowers on long stalks, found only in the Carolinas and Japan—and the largest and finest specimens of hemlock, cherry, and Fraser's magnolia in the United States. A 425-year-old hemlock tree was cut when the Highlands golf course was laid out in the 1920s. The growth rings of the trunk were dated back to 1503, the date of the last voyage of Christopher Columbus.

Even the shape and scope of the land itself proved rare in its dramatic display. Just northwest of Highlands, along a leg of U.S. Highway 64 from Franklin, North Carolina, is a series of spectacular waterfalls.

At Bridal Veil Falls, the water from which drops over the highway itself, cars may actually drive under the falls. At Dry Falls, visitors may stand on a walkway under the falls and, while staying dry, view through the sheet of falling water the Cullasaja River below. Low Falls is visible as the route descends into the Cullasaja Gorge.

The highway is carved out of perpendicular cliffs and frequently overlooks the river nestled in its gorge 250 feet below. It remains one of those places in North Carolina where you might be more comfortable on a mule than in a car. You can honestly say the view along this drive takes your breath away.

Before postcards could be made, Kelsey and Hutchinson set the task of building themselves homes that would serve as models for mountain dwellings. Once these were built, they figured, the town of Highlands would surely grow. They used massive, hand-squared logs placed upright to form the walls like a stockade around a fort. They nailed up clapboard on the outside and weatherboard in the interior.

To lure people to their new resort town, already the site of two fine homes, Kelsey and Hutchinson bombarded Kansas and the New England states with advertisements and brochures. In so doing, they created not only a town, but a problem as well.

Those who are not familiar with the politics of Bleeding Kansas around the time of the War Between the States should be reminded that by all standards Kansans were Yankees. They fought a fierce guerrilla war against Confederate sympathizers along the Missouri border. Within two years of the founding of Highlands, more than a dozen families from pro-Union backgrounds moved into the town atop the plateau just this side of Georgia. T. Baxter White came from Massachusetts to be named Highlands's first postmaster, while Judson M. Cobb of Wisconsin brought the first Jersey cattle.

Hutchinson didn't stick around long enough to witness the trouble. He moved his family back to the town in Kansas that already bore his name. Kelsey remained for quite a few years before moving to build another western North Carolina town, Linville.

While Highlands didn't develop into the trading center its founding fathers had dreamed it would, it did grow into one of the most beautiful and most popular resort towns in the mountains. A church and a school were erected. The first hotel, built in 1879, still stands today.

The influx of Yankees into the Confederate South brought bad feelings, though. A nearby community ultimately declared war on Highlands and blockaded the only road into town.

The lush, green town planted where X marked the spot was to be tested in 1883 by the three Xs associated with a jug of moonshine.

One of the prejudices the Yankee patriarchs brought to Highlands with their families and their cattle was their devotion to temperance. The town fathers of Highlands were uncompromisingly opposed to the use of intoxicating liquors. Their sons, however, proved quick to adopt the habits of mountain Southerners. And the trouble began.

Just across the state line in Rabun County, Georgia, cooking and drinking homemade whiskey was a way of life that had flourished since the area's earliest settlers. The moonshiners found a ready market for their alcohol among the young men of Highlands. This infuriated the town elders, who viewed the trafficking of whiskey as an influence that would turn their remote mountain village into a modern Gomorrah. Sodom, in their opinion, already existed in the Moccasin Township in Rabun County, Georgia.

Because the established local legal system had already been circumvented by moonshiners, the Highlands founding fathers sought the assistance of federal agents. These agents were known as "revenuers" because the federal crime associated with selling moonshine was the failure to pay taxes on a highly lucrative and highly taxable commodity. Next to veterans of Sherman's destructive march through the South, revenuers were the most unwelcome of all men in the mountains of Georgia and western North Carolina.

Revenuers swarmed into the area, smashing stills. The federal agents secured indictments against many of the violators, but they had limited power to make arrests themselves. This left the moonshiners free to continue cooking and selling corn whiskey until their trials.

Under federal pressure, the newly elected Rabun County sheriff began to arrest moonshiners who refused to leave the county. A hard-core cadre of moonshiners, led by four brothers named Billingsly, withstood all pressure. They had the reputation of being men whose rifles and squirrel guns were the law in their neck of the woods. They placed little value on the lives of those they saw as trespassers, especially those cursed revenuers.

Two men arrested by federal agents were brought to Highlands, the nearest town, and held in the Smith Hotel to await their trials. One of them had been arrested for moonshining and the other for attempting to effect the escape of the first.

News got back to Rabun County. And the Billingsly brothers literally declared war on Highlands.

They gathered to map out their campaign. One of the brothers penned an official declaration of war and sent it to Highlands by messenger. It warned the citizens that the Army of Moccasin would march on Highlands if the two arrested Georgians continued to be held.

The moonshiners were not released. Eighteen moonshiners from Georgia marched on Highlands, led by the Billingsly boys. They bivouacked behind a store directly across the street from the Smith Hotel, where the townsfolk had soberly barricaded themselves with the prisoners upon receiving the Georgians' declaration of war.

The siege continued for three days, the air filled with the crack of rifle fire as the forces engaged in nearly constant sharpshooting. Aim was taken on every head that appeared either behind the building or in the shot-out windows of the Smith Hotel. The Highlands men did not send a messenger for reinforcements because they figured he'd be shot trying to leave the hotel.

As it was, a Highlands man fired the only fatal shot of the three-day war. The Army of Moccasin had the audacity to spend the night flaunting their drinking of moonshine between volleys of rifle fire. A member of the makeshift army would dart between two buildings and into the street, take a swig of homemade liquor, let out a piercing rebel yell, and run quickly to cover. Tom Ford, a native mountaineer holed up with the townsfolk, was angered by this insulting display and by the situation as a whole. He climbed to the roof of the Smith Hotel at the end of the third day and shot dead one of the Billingsly gang, a man named Ramey.

A heavy stillness fell over the town as all shooting suddenly ceased. The Billingsly band withdrew, leaving behind a letter that stated they were returning to Georgia to bury their fallen patriot. They vowed to return with reinforcements to wage their war to the bitter end.

During the interim, Highlands sent runners to nearby towns, including Cashiers and Whiteside Cove, to ask for help. A large number of men and boys rushed to Highlands to defend the town against the next attack.

It never came.

Instead of an attack, the Billingsly brothers wrote another letter to the people of Highlands. The letter pointed out what was already known, that the road to Highlands passed through the center of Moccasin Township in Georgia. The Georgians announced a blockade that would cut off all supplies to the town. Instead of renewing hostilities in Highlands, the moonshiners vowed to kill any and every man from Highlands who attempted to pass over the Georgia road.

The threat was accepted as a sincere one. Not until the blockade had completely emptied the Highlands larders did anyone attempt to use the road. Finally, a man named Joel Lovin hitched his team to a wagon in hopes of traversing the road through Georgia to Walhalla, South Carolina, where he would pick up a load of desperately needed supplies for the town. He left in the rain.

The blockade had been punishment enough in the eyes of the moonshiners of Rabun County, apparently. As Joel Lovin drove his team of horses along the slick, muddy road, he was happened upon by the Billingsly brothers themselves. Though heavily armed, the Georgia moonshiners never so much as looked at the man from Highlands from under their wet slouch hats. The war was over.

A full sixteen years before Carry Nation went on her famous bottle-smashing rampages with a hatchet—in Kansas, ironically—temperance fighters waged an important battle in Highlands, North Carolina, a town founded by two Kansans who penciled an *X* on a map and refused to let a hostile terrain divert them from their dream.

Yet the spirit (and spirits) of the Southern moonshiners lived on. Illegal stills remained a backbone of the rural economy in depressed mountain areas in western North Carolina and all of Appalachia through Prohibition and into the late 1950s, until the high cost of sugar and lessening demand made cooking moonshine unprofitable. Yet even today there remain a few holes in the steep, green woods surrounding Highlands, North Carolina, where a revenuer remains as unwelcome as he was in 1883.

AN UNREAD LETTER
FROM THE ANCIENT PAST
· · · · · · · · · · · ·
· ·

Imagine receiving a one-page letter made of stone and larger than a king-size bed.

Such an ancient letter can actually be found in a farmer's field in the Nantahala National Forest in Jackson County, North Carolina, a pastoral area of lush green valleys. A state landmark sign posts a turnoff on the Caney Fork Road a little more than three miles off Highway 107 just south of East Laport. A state-erected shelter preserves Judaculla Rock, and thousands have come to touch the worn edges of an ancient and unknown America.

Judaculla Rock sits in the earth at a forty-five-degree angle, making a perfect writing table were you of extraordinary size. Judaculla is, in fact, the anglicized version of the name of the mythological Cherokee giant Tsul-Kalu, which means "His eyes are slanted." Judaculla is commonly translated as "slant-eyed giant." The rock is covered with carved "writings" from the otherworld, yet ancient Cherokee were no better able to translate their message than the many who have tried since.

One anthropologist insisted that the writings were the record and resulting treaty of a battle fought between the Cherokee and the Creeks in Georgia in 1775. He claimed that certain figures on the rock—a bird here, a fish there—represented fallen Cherokee warriors. Perhaps this anthropologist had read too many buffalo hides and teepees of the Plains Indians, who were quite adept at such pictographic paintings of battles. Southern Cherokee did not record such things in rock carvings.

Other scientists visited Judaculla Rock after the anthropologist published his claims, and it was determined that the carvings had been made long before the American Revolution. It is believed that the writings were executed before the Cherokee even inhabited the area, that they may be as old as the ash-and-water drawings of the cavemen who lived toward the end of the Ice Age. Judaculla Rock may have been in place when early men chased wooly mammoths into huge rock pits.

The markings on Judaculla Rock invite misinterpretation. Where some see an owl, others see a fish. Still others would interpret the fish as a symbol for man. Dominating the multitude of symbols on the rock is what appears to be the imprint of a human hand with seven fingers, a hand so large it must have been that of a giant.

It is necessary to understand the Cherokee belief system to appreciate their traditional myth of Judaculla Rock. In the Cherokee system, the physical world was closely paralleled by the spiritual world. All things possessed a spirit—men, deer, trees, wind—and these spirits were controlled by gods which often appeared in the physical world as oversized, powerful examples of the things they represented in the world of the spirits. In turn, these gods were under the control of the Great Being.

The Cherokee believed that they died two deaths, a death of the body and a death of the spirit. Since the death of the spirit was of greater importance, the Cherokee needed a mediator with the celestial beings, someone who could save their spirits and lift them to the heavens, where they would live eternally. Judaculla Rock is the relic of one such mediator.

Their spiritual mediator was one of their own, a beloved daughter of the Cherokee. She lived at a time before people were given names. In fact, all these events took place before the Cherokee kept a narrative history of ancestry passed from one generation to the next. For as long as all Cherokee can remember, the Judaculla Rock has existed where it exists today as a chronicle of the Cherokee's union with the world of the spirits.

In ancient Cherokee times, there was a girl who lived with her widowed mother and a brother. Her brother was a brave and fierce warrior but a poor hunter. In times of battle, the family was the home of a hero. At other times, they depended on handouts to be able to eat.

The girl was enchanted one summer day by a babbling brook in the Balsam Mountains. It beckoned her with its haunting sound and the golden sparkle of its tumbling waters. She followed the stream high into the mountains until she came upon a sun-drenched glen of blossoming azaleas, laurels, and rhododendrons. Her spirit sang to be among such beauty.

She sat down at the edge of the crystal stream and only then realized how tired she'd become from her long walk up the mountain. She laid her dark hair on a pillow of springy moss and fell asleep. Immediately, she began to dream. By dreaming in this, a magic place, she entered the world of the spirits.

Inside the world filled with the mists of a thousand mountain mornings, she felt the gentle touch of another spirit. The spirit of her dream appeared then beside her, and she felt the stirrings of her womanhood. He was handsome and graceful, strong and lithe, and he sang to her in rich and pleasing tones. The girl realized she was being seduced and asked him to stop.

The spirit smiled kindly, and his eyes danced with great pleasure. He proposed marriage to her on the spot. The girl told her spirit suitor that her mother would let her marry no one but a good hunter, because her mother was a widow and because the girl had only one brother, and he was a warrior. The spirit laughed with delight upon hearing this. In a deep, resounding voice he proclaimed, "I am a great hunter."

He certainly was that, for the spirit was the god of the hunt. The maiden gave herself to him, and they were married. A gentle breeze of the spirit world caressed her from that day forward.

Back in the physical world, things weren't going so well. The maiden's disappearance caused grave concern among the Cherokee. The people of her camp searched throughout the neighboring Cherokee villages and concluded that the girl had been abducted by other Indians. Whipped into a state of agitation by the maiden's brother, her people declared war on the neighboring tribes. Villages were invaded and many battles were fought in an effort to find her place of concealment and bring her back to her village.

The new bride watched from the spirit world and was grieved by the bloodshed and sorrow brought on by the war. She sent away the breeze that comforted her and pleaded with her husband, the guardian of the eternal hunting grounds, to do something for her people. Holding dominion over the hunt in the physical world, he sent a large stag to deliver a message to the people of her village. The deer told them that the missing daughter could be found only if her mother and brother went to a special place in the woods, at the edge of a mountain by a gurgling creek, and fasted for seven days.

This put an end to the bloody battles, and the mother and her warrior son did as they were told. They followed the deer to a secluded spot in the woods where two creeks branched from one.

There they fasted for six days, singing songs to the world of the spirits. On the sixth day, their singing was answered by the sound of a drum and the vision of a cave opening in the side of the mountain.

The son was convinced that the vision meant their fasting was a success, and he asked the stag if he could eat, for he had traveled many days and he was very hungry. The deer only repeated the original instructions. It was clear that the mother and son must fast one more day.

Soon the drumming intensified, and a campfire lighted the inside of the cave. The mother and son watched in awe the dancing of the spirits of the otherworld. The spirits were beautiful and graceful, casting long shadows on the walls of the cave. The mother and son saw that the girl was one of the spirits, dancing happily with the others. At the end of the seventh day, the widow and her son were to be permitted to enter the cave, to join the world of the spirits, and to talk with the new wife.

But the girl's brother believed that the fast was over upon seeing his sister dancing happily in the cave. By then he was nearly starving, so weak he believed he might die if he didn't eat. The young warrior brought out some dried meat they had carried with them. His mother screamed for him to stop. Instead, the warrior stuffed the meat into his mouth and began to chew. The drumming faded, the dancers disappeared, and the campfire inside the cave went out. And, as he swallowed his first bite, the mountain closed again, sealing the cave.

All that the son and his mother could hear then was the rushing of water in the creek.

The god of the hunt, the girl's husband of the spirit world, was so angered by this disobedience that he entered the physical world, appearing as Judaculla, the slant-eyed giant. His physical manifestation was huge, ugly, and frightening. He towered above the son and threw lightning from his hands, shouting words of anger. His voice was the roaring thunder of storm clouds. The young warrior and his mother fled.

The entire village gathered to hear their story. The finest warriors and hunters were led to the place of the magic cave carrying weapons of war. A large rock now stood where the cave had been. It was Judaculla's rock, the spirit's stepping-stone into the physical world of mortal beings.

The Cherokee villagers began to chant battle songs and dance the dance of war. This further angered the god of the hunt, and he appeared once more as Judaculla, as big and as ugly as before. The Cherokee men fell silent in terror, as thunderbolts and great flashes of lightning filled the sky. Judaculla's wrath threatened to split the mountain in two.

The warrior brother was himself enraged, realizing that his sister was alive in the spirit world and that Judaculla was keeping her from him. He lifted his club and raised a war whoop from deep inside his body, challenging the giant. Judaculla lost his temper and threw a bolt of lightning through the young warrior, killing him before the echo of his cry died. The Cherokee men ran to their village to tell the widow she had lost her son.

The new bride of the spirit world was so grieved by the death of her brother that she could not stop weeping. This saddened all the spirits, especially her husband. She confronted him and said she could no longer live in the world of the spirits. She prepared to return to the village to live out her mortal life at her mother's side.

To keep his new wife, the god of the hunt decided to give to her people a gift of reconciliation that would benefit them and their children forever. He granted all brave warriors, proud hunters, and faithful wives an eternal home in the world of the spirits upon their deaths. The god of the hunt thus became the guardian spirit of the Cherokee. The bride was soon joined by the spirit of her fallen brother.

The caressing breeze returned to the bride and became her constant companion. This mediator between the Cherokee and the world of the spirits has always appeared in subsequent visions with long, raven hair lifting in her accompanying breeze.

From that day on, all Cherokee enjoyed the eternal life of the spirits by living honest lives and demonstrating their strength of heart to the god of the hunt.

When the villagers returned to retrieve the body of the fallen brother, they discovered the writing on Judaculla Rock. They could not read the messages there, but it was understood that the writing told the way a man may enter the world of the spirits. The ground was declared sacred. A stag appeared from the woods and told the Cherokee that they must never hunt in the area marked by Judaculla's rock.

All the elders and the young men agreed that this should be so. But as time went by, one winter when game was scarce two young hunters attempted to shoot a deer on the sacred mountain. Judaculla appeared in a rage and chased the hunters. Just as he was about to grab them in his seven-fingered hand, he slipped at the bottom of the hill and his reach fell short. The god of the hunt left the imprint of his giant hand on Judaculla Rock. The handprint served as an emphatic warning against the taking of game from the sacred area.

The carved messages of Judaculla Rock remain a mystery today. It is still claimed that a faithful Cherokee may fast for seven days at the site of the stone. If his singing is enjoyed by the spirits of the otherworld, he will be able to read the message on the rock. Only then will he understand the instructions for how a mortal man enters the world of the spirits.

BIGFOOT OF THE BALSAMS

A s the Abominable Snowman haunts the Himalayas, Boojum hides in the woods near Eagle Nest Mountain at the edge of the Plott Balsams in Haywood County.

Boojum was said to be larger than a bear, and just as hairy. Some believed he was a man raised by bears. Others suggested he was born of a female bear. All agreed, however, that he was at least partially human. He was not, by all accounts, pretty to look at.

Half-man, half-beast, Boojum was relentlessly hunted by guests of the famous Eagle Nest Hotel, a resort that catered to hay-fever sufferers at the turn of the century. Perched atop a mile-high peak that looked down upon Waynesville, the Eagle Nest Hotel was the starting point for numerous organized expeditions to search for Boojum and the treasure he was rumored to have hidden in the caves.

Boojum was a well-established reality to the guests of the mountain resort by 1906, when Peter G. Thompson visited the Eagle Nest Hotel. Thompson, it has been recorded, was responsible for spreading the story of Boojum outside the area of the

North Carolina mountains, a story that included a cache of valuable jewels hoarded by the giant beast.

Boojum was obsessed with collecting mountain jewels, the small precious stones found in western North Carolina. He was said to have spent his entire life hunting gems, and most believed he accumulated a fortune in rubies, emeralds, beryls, and amethysts. He was said to have hidden his cache in a mountain cave.

Leagues of fortune seekers scoured Eagle Nest Mountain in search of the cave. They came on horseback in the summer and left only after the last brittle leaves of autumn had fallen from the trees. Many treasure hunters claimed to have caught glimpses of Boojum, but they were very likely seeing bears in the distant undergrowth. Still, such spottings attracted frantic searches for days to come, the bears long gone and unaware of the ruckus they'd instigated.

Locals rarely made this mistake. They knew that Boojum was heard more often than he was seen. He constantly moaned as he searched for jewels, singing a deep, scratchy song of guttural howls and whines.

Despite his fear of human contact, the hairy giant exhibited a fondness for women. Though he was able to hide himself in the dense forest at will, Boojum occasionally approached a woman who found herself alone in the woods.

In warm weather, it wasn't rare for a mountain woman to bathe in one of the many creeks or pools tucked away in the forest, hidden from prying eyes by the dense undergrowth. At the peak of the summer heat, young girls were fond of swimming in the buff whenever they believed no one was around to watch.

It was as if Boojum could hear them taking off their clothes. His ears were specially tuned, it seemed, to the sound of a woman's voice and the noise a body makes splashing around in water.

These were the only times Boojum was ever seen in daylight. Covered with greasy, matted hair, he frightened bathers by appearing suddenly at the water's edge. His broken-toothed mouth agape, Boojum would watch a bathing woman for quite some time, the silence broken only by his breathing. Then he would turn with a small moan or sigh and lumber off into the trees. The female bather was left to clamber quickly out of the water, find her clothes, and rush home with the terrible story of how she was nearly attacked by the hairy giant of Eagle Nest Mountain.

Eventually, Boojum stumbled upon a woman who was not frightened by his horrible appearance. Her name was Annie.

An attractive woman, Annie was drawn by Boojum's sad eyes. She said that there was no reason a man should be so sad—if indeed Boojum was a man at all. Annie became his friend and his companion in the forested outback. She grew quite fond of Boojum, so different was he from other men. Boojum obviously enjoyed Annie's friendship as well, but their companionship did not diminish his love of bright, sparkling gemstones. From time to time, Boojum disappeared for days, leaving Annie to fend for herself while he searched for jewels.

When a mountain girl gives her heart, she gives it for good. An awful lonesomeness overtook Annie at these times, a lonesomeness she'd never known before. She'd fight all day to conquer her sorrow. But by nightfall she'd give in to her yearning and set off into the hollows searching for Boojum.

She called to him with a singularly haunting song of love, a cry of longing that would inspire Boojum to respond with his own mournful call and return to her. There were many times that it took Annie more than one night's searching to find Boojum, who might be just about anywhere in the mountains.

Guests of the Eagle Nest Hotel said that Annie's baleful song resembled the hoot of an owl. Annie was often heard carrying on in the night woods, and it wasn't long before she became known as Hootin' Annie. John Parris, a North Carolina columnist and folklorist, claimed that this was the origin of the expression "hootenanny." In the 1960s, a hootenanny came to be known as a party that centered on music, singing, and an all-around general whooping it up.

After many months, Annie finally persuaded Boojum to marry her. Occasionally, they took up residence in her nearby cabin. More often, she traveled with Boojum through the forest, moving from one cave to the next as he gathered valuable gems from the mountainsides. It is not known whether Annie ever became a mother. Some believe that she did, because something that looks very much like Boojum is said to reside in the area today. Local womenfolk are still warned not to swim alone in secluded streams and pools.

Boojum's collection of valuable gems has yet to be found. Some say that Annie buried the jewels along with her man when Boojum died one cold winter from exposure. Another theory is that Annie sent a package containing the fortune in gems to her kin just before she died. Even today, locals continue to thoroughly search any caves they discover on forays onto Eagle Nest Mountain.

FAIRY CROSSES AND
THE IMMORTAL NUNNEHI

A mong the grandeur of the ancient and expansive mountain ranges of western North Carolina are small things a visitor should not overlook.

Sprinkled in the midst of large rock formations, cascading waterfalls, steep valleys and gorges, and towering trees are occasional small bursts of color. Rubies and other gemstones may be found throughout the area. If one looks closely enough, red, orange, white, and yellow mushrooms can be seen brightening the underbrush.

Populating the folklore of the Cherokee are numerous little people who were an integral part of the abundant small life of the mountain forests. These include the Nunnehi immortals and the mysterious moon-eyed people.

The Nunnehi were invisible at will and could be seen when they wanted to be. Though spirits akin to mountain fairies, the Nunnehi at times resembled the Cherokee Indians in the way they acted and spoke.

The Nunnehi lived throughout the mountains, but they are most closely associated with the town of Franklin. Franklin, the seat of Macon County, overlooks the valley of the Little Tennessee River from its altitude of 2,113 feet. It was built on the site of the sacred Cherokee city of Nikwasi, near which the noted Indian Mound can still be found, the mound that supported the sacred house where important Indian councils were held. The Cherokee did not construct Indian Mound, however. They claimed that a perpetual flame burned within the mound, which was the home of the Nunnehi.

Like other fairies around the world, the Nunnehi much enjoyed music and dancing. But it was a rare instance when a Cherokee hunter happened to catch a glimpse of the spirited forest festivals of the Nunnehi. Hunters in the mountains did report, though, hearing the dance songs and the drums. Yet when an Indian approached the party, it seemed to move. Then the noise would mysteriously be heard behind the befuddled hunters or in the distance in another direction altogether. Cherokee hunters ran themselves in circles in search of the source of the Nunnehi music.

Though the Nunnehi were considered friendly, an Indian never attended one of their dances without being invited.

The Nunnehi were credited with assisting Cherokee who were lost in the forest, particularly in winter. The Nunnehi on these occasions would appear from their world of invisibility to bring the lost person inside their town houses under the mountains. There the lost soul would be rested and warmed. Once revived, the lost Indian would be guided back to the Cherokee village.

The Nunnehi did more than offer comfort to the lost Indian in the winter mountains. More than once or twice the Nunnehi warriors also came out of hiding to help the Cherokee in battle whenever it seemed the Cherokee might be losing. In fact, the

Nunnehi saved the Cherokee from defeat in the defense of Nikwasi, present-day Franklin.

In the rich folklore of the Cherokee there is a story told by a respected elder of an eerie experience he had in the mountainous Nantahala Forest when he was a boy of ten. Bored with practicing his bow and arrow, the boy was building a fish trap in the river by stacking stones into two long walls across the water. A stranger approached and watched him lifting and carrying the heavy stones. As the boy tired, the stranger suggested he needed a rest and invited him to walk upriver, where there was plenty to eat at the stranger's house if the boy was hungry. He was.

The boy accompanied the stranger. Inside the home, the stranger's wife was preparing dinner for a group of people. All were strangers to the boy, but they were pleased that the youngster had come for dinner. Still, the boy was apprehensive, and this was apparent to the adults.

To show the young Cherokee that they meant him no harm, the strangers invited in a man the boy knew. It was Udsi-skala, a friend of the boy's father. With Udsi-skala present, the boy decided that it must be all right for him to stay, and the entire group enjoyed a fine meal. Tired and well-fed, the boy fell contentedly asleep by the fire.

In the morning, he awoke unafraid, though Udsi-skala was no longer there. After breakfast, the stranger and the boy set out down a path toward the boy's home. There was a field of golden corn on one side of the path and a peach orchard on the other. They soon came upon another trail, and the stranger told the boy to follow it to the river.

The young Cherokee knew the river would lead him home. The stranger said good-bye and turned back along the orchard trail toward his home as the boy walked the trail that led to the river. After a short distance, the youngster realized he'd forgotten to thank the stranger for his hospitality. He turned around to do so and discovered that the stranger had already disappeared from sight. The boy ran back along the trail a short distance to catch up to the stranger, then stopped abruptly, seeing that there was no longer a cornfield on one side of the path. Spinning on his heels, the boy saw the peach orchard had disappeared from the landscape as well.

The boy didn't realize it, but he had just returned from the invisible land of the Nunnehi.

He made his way to his village and learned that his people had searched for him throughout the night. The boy's family was worried that he had drowned in the river. Embarrassed by the trouble he'd caused, the youth quickly explained where he'd been. He said that since he had seen Udsi-skala, he assumed his parents would be told where he was.

Udsi-skala was among the villagers who had gathered upon the boy's return. He quickly stepped forward.

"I was out all night in my canoe, looking for you," he told the boy. "It was one of the Nunnehi who made himself look like me."

With his family and other villagers, the boy returned to the place where he'd spent the night. They searched the entire area on both sides of the ridge, but a house was never located. Neither was the cornfield, nor the orchard of peach trees. It was agreed by all that the Nunnehi had taken on the appearance of Cherokee Indians in an effort to make the youth comfortable.

The Nunnehi so enjoyed music that they sometimes attended the dances of the Cherokee. On one occasion, four attractive women dropped by a Cherokee dance. It was assumed that they were from another village and were drawn to the party by the music.

The women proved popular and lively dancers, attracting the attention of several Indian bachelors. It was very late when the dancing finally ended, and four young Cherokee volunteered to walk the women home to guarantee their safety through the forest at night. The young men followed the pretty women at a respectful distance on the trail. Then the four Cherokee men stood aghast as they watched the visiting dancers walk into the river and disappear before their eyes. One of the Indians beat the water with his hands out of frustration while the others searched the area.

The women were Nunnehi who lived under the river and who had taken on the appearance of Cherokee because they so loved dancing.

Since the Nunnehi were believed to be immortal, some have suggested that they were the spirits of dead Cherokee. This assumption is incorrect because the Nunnehi inhabited the Nantahala National Forest long before the arrival of the Cherokee. And if mountain folklore is to be believed, they will continue to live under the mountains and streams long after the Cherokee are gone.

Numerous other diminutive spirits and fairies were believed to dwell in the forested mountains.

The moon-eyed people were a race of men much smaller than the Cherokee, with white skin, bearded faces, and blue eyes. They lived in the mountains of Tennessee and North Carolina. According to Cherokee legend, the moon-eyed people inhabited the area long before the Spaniards came in search of gold. The Cherokee knew of their existence because of a line of fortifications constructed by the moon-eyed people, a series of small mounds and stacked rocks arranged from one end of the region to the other.

The moon-eyed people dwelt in small, rounded houses of branches and mud. Blinded by sunlight, they only came out at night to hunt, fish, and gather food. During a full moon, they were as blind as in daylight.

The warring Creeks, it was said, journeyed from the south to drive the little people from their homeland during a full moon. This happened at a time before history, according to the Cherokee. It remains forever a mystery where the moon-eyed people went.

There do exist a number of crumbling mounds and fortifications that the Cherokee disclaim. It is quite possible that there was a race of native Americans living in the area before the Cherokee arrived from the southeast. Whatever primitive race of humans inhabited the mountains of western North Carolina before the Cherokee, it is the vague legend of the moon-eyed people that remains their legacy.

The Yunwi Tsusdi, or Little People, are sometimes confused by folklorists with the Nunnehi, though the Yunwi Tsusdi never took on the appearance of people as did the Nunnehi.

These Little People, while generally friendly, did not like to be followed. No taller than a normal Cherokee's knee, the handsome, long-haired Little People kept their houses and towns secret—with a vengeance. The Yunwi Tsusdi so valued their privacy that they were known to put death curses on any Cherokee who located one of their homes and revealed its location to another Indian. The folklore of the Cherokee includes stories of villagers who died after revealing the location of a dwelling place of the Yunwi Tsusdi.

Other Cherokee mountain fairies were individual spirits.

De-tsata was a small boy who ran into the woods to avoid a spanking. He has tried to keep himself invisible ever since. Reported to be handsome though very small, De-tsata spent most of his time hunting birds with his bow and arrow. He also fathered a great many children who were all just like him and were known by the same name.

Whenever a flock of birds flew up suddenly in the mountains, it was said that De-tsata was chasing them. Frequently, De-tsata proved mischievous and hid a bird hunter's arrow that missed its target. When a Cherokee hunter couldn't find his arrow, he shouted a threat to spank De-tsata unless the arrow was returned.

In these cases, the hunter then easily found the missing arrow.

Other Cherokee mountain fairies were Tsawasi and Tsagasi, who helped deer hunters by allowing them to sneak up on their prey without startling it. Though good-natured, these two fairies were held responsible whenever a Cherokee hunter slipped or fell in the forest. There were other fairy spirits who were not evil, but who were known to play tricks on the Cherokee.

For those who might be skeptical of the existence of the spirit people and fairies of western North Carolina, evidence has been left behind. Besides the mounds and the mysterious smoke rising from underground Nunnehi fireplaces, relics known as fairy crosses are sprinkled throughout the area. Found even to this day, fairy crosses are small crystals formed in the shape of a cross. Along with North Carolina gemstones, fairy crosses are polished to perfect symmetry and are valued additions to numerous gem and rock collections across the country.

Found in the largest numbers in Cherokee and Clay counties, fairy crosses are believed by some to be the crystallized tears of the Nunnehi. Others insist that the Nunnehi were able to make themselves visible and invisible at will because they each possessed a fairy cross, which they wore on strings around their necks. Nunnehi who lost their fairy crosses also lost the ability to become visible, and were destined to live in the invisible world beneath the rocks and water forever.

On the other hand, lucky is the person who finds a fairy cross lost by a Nunnehi. A person in possession of a fairy cross has the power, with the appropriate faith, to become invisible at will. It should be noted that fairy crosses sold in shops throughout the region are done so, however, without guarantee.

ULAGU,
THE GIANT YELLOW JACKET
·············
··

"The woods are lovely, dark, and deep," wrote Robert Frost in "Stopping by Woods on a Snowy Evening." He certainly wasn't thinking of Nantahala Gorge. There the woods are scary, dark, and steep.

Some of the most dramatically rugged scenery in western North Carolina can be found in the Nantahala Gorge, which runs along U.S. Highway 19 between Wesson and Nantahala in Swain and Macon counties. Cut ages ago by the Nantahala River, the gorge is so steep that it was called Land of the Middle Sun by the Cherokee because daylight reached the bottom of the gorge only when the midday sun was directly between the high cliffs on either side.

The bottom of the gorge was a dark and forbidding place where numerous monsters were known to dwell. One of the most ferocious beasts who lived there was a giant yellow jacket known as Ulagu, the Cherokee word for boss or leader.

Ulagu developed a taste for children. For many years, the yellow jacket terrorized the Cherokee by swooping down out of the sky to carry off children who were shocked into immobility by the suddenness of its attack. The appearance of Ulagu, its body as large as a house, was always accompanied by a wind created by the beast's huge wings. Its whirring flight drowned out all other forest sounds and was said to be as loud as a persistent roll of thunder.

Ulagu was also a rapid flyer. While the Cherokee men often tried to track the yellow jacket that was carrying off a screaming child to its secret hiding place, it always flew too swiftly to be followed.

In a desperate attempt to discover Ulagu's nest, the Cherokee set traps of fresh meat for the monster yellow jacket. White strings were tied around the meat. Cherokee hunters believed that Ulagu could be traced more easily with a string dangling from its clutches. Yet each time the horrific Ulagu carried away the meat, it darted so swiftly that the yellow jacket was out of sight before the string could be followed. The Cherokee hunters increased the size of both the bait and the string until a whole deer was finally offered. The meat was tied with a long string the thickness of a rope.

The giant yellow jacket returned once more and seized the bait. This time, however, the load proved heavy enough to slow Ulagu's flight and to cause the monster yellow jacket to fly much lower in the sky. The rope could be followed as it dangled just above the tops of the trees. A group of hunters pursued Ulagu along a high ridge, then watched as it flew across the gorge and disappeared into the side of the cliff opposite.

The hunters marked the spot in their minds where the white rope had disappeared into the face of the cliff. With a great shout, they ran down into the dark gorge and up the other side. There they discovered a hidden cave out of which a strong breeze blew, the air stirred by the working of Ulagu's enormous wings.

Standing outside, the hunters saw that the top of the cave was covered with a thick comb of six-sided chambers made from a waxy, papery material. The cave was teeming with yellow-colored wasps of normal size. Afraid they would be stung to death and eaten by Ulagu, the Cherokee hunters decided to kill the great beast and the smaller wasps by filling the cave with smoke.

A fire was built and tended at the mouth of the cave until the nest was entirely filled with choking smoke, killing Ulagu and most of the smaller yellow jackets. A few of the normal-sized wasps, though, managed to escape. According to Cherokee legend, the escaping wasps flew into the forest and multiplied until they lived everywhere in the world.

The offspring of Ulagu continue to be a stinging nuisance to people today. Whenever a Cherokee is stung by a wasp, he is likely to be reminded that long ago a much greater evil inhabited the earth. A visit to Nantahala Gorge inspires the feeling that when monsters inhabited our planet, they must have chosen the spookiest of places to live. And those who know the legend of Ulagu are apt to drive through the Land of the Middle Sun with the windows rolled up.

THE ENCHANTED LAKE
OF THE SMOKY MOUNTAINS
• • • • • • • • • • • •
• •

A mong the rugged recesses of the mountains is a wildlife refuge managed by a huge, white bear. At the center of animal paradise, near the foot of Clingman's Dome, is a magic lake that remains hidden among the rhododendron and beneath the towering trees.

Clingman's Dome, the highest point in the Great Smoky Mountains National Park at 6,642 feet, overlooks Newfound Gap in the heart of the Smokies. The mountain straddles the state line between Gatlinburg, Tennessee, and Cherokee, North Carolina.

A tree-covered peak named for Thomas Lanier Clingman, a Confederate general and United States senator, Clingman's Dome was known to early white settlers as Smoky Dome. It is the mountain made famous by the popular ballad "On Top of Old Smoky." Before becoming the site of latter-day lost love, Clingman's Dome reigned over a most magical area of the Smokies.

Known to the Cherokee Indians as Kuwa-Hi, which translates as "Mulberry Place," Clingman's Dome and two nearby mountains were considered the sacred home of the bears. The Cherokee respected bears above all other animals because bears were once human. It was believed the bears of North Carolina could talk if they wanted to. There are numerous Indian stories of hunters overhearing conversations between bears. At times, their words were even understandable. The bears, however, never spoke *to* the Cherokee. While it was within their power to do so, the bears chose simply to talk only among themselves.

Clingman's Dome was where all the bears of the forest returned each autumn to throw a huge party before turning in for the winter. The bears took this opportunity to tell their stories of the summer before. And many times the Cherokee hunters reported seeing the bears dancing in large groups at the time of winter's approach. The Indians left the bears at Clingman's Dome alone because it was there that the great leader of the bears also lived.

Much larger than any bear seen by man, the Great White Bear held dominion over the other bears. He also served as their advisor and medicine man. He devised a way to cure a bear of àny wound, even one that might otherwise have proven fatal. All a wounded bear needed do was make its way to Mulberry Place and submerge itself in the Enchanted Lake.

By swimming across the magic lake, a wounded bear came out on the other side healed and whole. The Cherokee say that bears traveled to Enchanted Lake through all hardships from hundreds of miles away to have wounds cured by a swim in the refreshing water of the secret lake.

The lake also provided curative powers to other animals, including birds. The Cherokee believed the Enchanted Lake would also cure a wounded man because the magic of the lake was so powerful.

Hidden in the forest recesses of balsam, spruce, hemlock, and rhododendron, the Enchanted Lake is located in the wildest region of the Smoky Mountains somewhere in the vicinity of the headwaters of Deep Creek in Swain County, North Carolina. While the Cherokee know the lake is there, no one living has ever seen it. This is not only because the trail is so difficult that only animals can find the Enchanted Lake, but because the Great White Bear cast a spell upon the lake to make it invisible to man.

Were it visible, the Enchanted Lake would prove too tempting to hunters. Its waters teem with fish and reptiles of every kind, and its surface is literally so crowded with waterfowl that thousands of ducks and geese hover in the air, awaiting their turn to swim. The flocks of waterfowl are so thick they block out the sun. The Cherokee call the magic lake Atag-Hi, which means "Place of Water Birds." Yet the Enchanted Lake belongs to the bears. Their tracks crisscross the shores of the sacred lake from every direction.

Atag-Hi appears to men as a low, flat place in the mountain valley. Where there is water, men cannot see water. Where there are tracks, men see only the undisturbed forest floor. Where there are huge flocks of birds in the sky, men see only sunshine or thin wisps of clouds floating among the distant shapes of the Smoky Mountains.

According to Cherokee legend, there was a young man who in his heart did not wish to harm the bears or the birds, who did not desire to hunt the deer or eat the fish from the magic water of the Enchanted Lake. To this man, the secret lake appeared.

The young Indian of good intentions fasted for days at the place he believed the lake to be. He sang prayers throughout the night without sleep, and the lake appeared to him at daybreak. It appeared as a wide expanse of glistening, violet water. The waters that fed the lake from high cliffs overhead were revealed to him as clear waterfalls with a violet tint thundering down over the rocks. His spiritual vision sharpened by vigil and prayer, the young man witnessed the great multitude of birds, fish, rabbits, and deer at

Atag-Hi. And he was able to understand what the bears said to each other as they swam across the Enchanted Lake. One mother bear told her cub the direction to turn in a streambed when the approach of a man was heard.

As the lifting sun burned through the morning mist of the Smoky Mountains, the Enchanted Lake began to disappear. Realizing the lake was fading, the young Indian marked the place with a small pile of stones. The Cherokee hunter was pleased with his vision and spoke often of the sacred lake kept by the Great White Bear at the foot of Clingman's Dome.

An extremely severe winter followed. Hunting was greatly hampered by snow and ice that coated the mountains. A savage wind howled constantly, freezing a hunter's fingers as he drew back an arrow on his bow. Game was scarce. The mountain animals huddled in protective recesses, rarely venturing out into the rampages of the weather.

The Cherokee village soon suffered a shortage of food. A council was held and it was decided that the young visionary must hunt the Enchanted Lake to keep his people from starving. It was contrary to the young Indian's vision to do so, but the hunger of his own family convinced him to try to take meat from Atag-Hi.

The young man bundled up and walked through a virtual blizzard, among aged trees collapsed into broken heaps under the weight of ice and snow. Coming to the place of his vision, he sat under a Carolina hemlock, a tree that provides excellent cover from the weather. He leaned his back against the thick, deeply furrowed bark of the trunk. Looking out from under his cover of short, drooping branches, he sang his prayers through the coldest night of his life.

By morning, the wind had died. Sunshine sparkled brightly off the ice and snow. Warm mist lifted from the waters of the Enchanted Lake, which the young hunter could plainly see. Animals and birds were in magnificent abundance. He slipped out his bow and, stepping from inside the cover of the hemlock, fired an arrow into one of the nearby bears.

The Cherokee figured it was best to kill the animal that would provide his village the most meat. Struck in the neck, the bear spun awkwardly to see where the shot had come from. He groaned in surprise and pain, then spoke clearly to the young hunter.

The howling of the wind stopped. The thousands of birds upon the lake kept still. The deer held their places, and the rabbits did not move. The other bears stared at the young hunter. It did not seem possible that a man had invaded their magical sanctuary.

The wounded bear told the hunter that he had betrayed his vision. The Cherokee was then set upon by the other bears and killed. The wounded bear fell into the purple waters of the lake and was perfectly healed.

When the weather cleared days later, men from the village found the torn body of the young hunter. It was laying in a clearing, a low, flat place the elders said had once been a marsh. Though the hunter had been torn to pieces by the claws and teeth of many bears, the villagers did not find a single track in the snow.

The hunter's treachery so angered the Great White Bear that he will now allow no man to see the Enchanted Lake, no matter how diligently he prays or how long he fasts. Locating the magic lake is not as impossible as it may seem, however. At certain times, the furious beating of thousands upon thousands of wings may be heard as birds land on or lift from the surface of the magic lake.

Some claim that morning mist rising from the lake can be seen from the peak of Clingman's Dome, from the top of Old Smoky. And an occasional old-timer in northern Swain County has been known to show a curious visitor the spot where he once found a water-lily blossom hung up in the needles of a Carolina hemlock, or trapped among the interlocking tendrils of a mountain rhododendron near the foot of Clingman's Dome.

THE MURDERED HERMIT
•••••••••••••
••

There are places in the mountains of western North Carolina where, for no known reason, trees refuse to grow. Large areas void of trees in the otherwise woods-covered mountains are known as balds.

Balds do support plant life, and they should not be confused with outcroppings of exposed rock like those on Whiteside Mountain. Balds are simply naturally bare of forests. There are two basic types of balds, with dozens of variations. Those covered by a combination of grasses, weed clumps, and wild flowers are called grass balds. Those that support shrubs are called heath balds. Such treeless areas are found only in the southern reaches of the Appalachian Mountains.

Scientists have adequately "diagnosed" the balds, yet they have failed to sustain a single theory to explain their cause. No one has explained why balds, occurring at altitudes from two thousand to six thousand feet, will not support trees. Altitude is not the answer, since nearby mountains at similar altitudes support an abundance of trees. Upon examination, the soil of the balds has proven adequate to support the growth of trees.

In 1938, Dr. W. A. Gates, a Louisiana State University professor, offered an interesting theory in his attempt to explain the balds. Having discovered that a particular species of wasp was responsible for the death of some oak trees in the mountains, Gates claimed that the wasps were responsible for creating the balds. The egg-laying process of this wasp did kill a few oak trees under his observation, yet new questions presented themselves. It remained to be explained, for example, why healthy trees grow to the precise edges of some established balds. Wasp infestations spread from tree to tree as long as the wasps remain active, but tree growth returns to the area once they are eradicated or move to another location. So, Gates's theory does not explain the permanence of balds.

Indians in the area were fascinated by balds, creating reasons for their existence and stories behind their creation. Among the superstitious mountain settlers who followed, the devil figured prominently in explanations of the mysterious balds. According to tradition, the balds were created when the devil went walking through the mountains, each of his footfalls resulting in a tract of stunted growth.

Every major bald in the mountains has at least one story to tell. The story of Grier's Bald is based on documented fact. It centers around a man as strongly feared as the devil himself, a fear that ultimately worked against him and cost him his life.

Just inside the Tennessee line off U.S. Highway 23 north of Asheville, Big Bald Mountain is easily spotted. Traversed by the Appalachian Trail, Big Bald rises to 5,530 feet at the border between Madison and Yancey counties. Topped by a large expanse of sparse shrubbery thickets, Big Bald is known locally as Grier's Bald.

David Grier was a hermit who lived on Big Bald from 1802 until his death more than thirty years later. When exploring American folklore, one is struck by the large number of hermits who took off for the hills after disappointments in love. Such was the case with Grier, who was rejected by the daughter of Colonel David Vance. Grier lived at first in a cave near the summit of Big Bald. Eventually, he erected a small log cabin nearby, next to a large spring that can still be found.

Soon after moving into the cave, Grier proclaimed himself king of the mountain. Living the life of a "literary" recluse, he is said to have penned a work on religion in addition to his better-known opus, a treatise on human government, particularly as it applied to Big Bald Mountain. Grier announced that all visitors and anyone who wanted to become his neighbor must submit to the "laws" he enacted.

As self-appointed king, Grier refused to pay taxes. When he was called into court over a poll-tax bill of seventy-five cents, he pelted the courthouse windows with stones. Rifle in hand, the hermit chased the judge and lawyers from the building and drove them into hiding. King Grier then returned to his mountain.

He became involved in a number of heated disputes when settlers encroached upon his dominion. He was said to amuse himself by mutilating any cattle he discovered wandering within his kingdom. Eventually, Grier killed a man. In broad daylight and in cold blood, David Grier shot a man named Higgins, whose only offense was to hunt deer on land over which Grier had proclaimed dominion.

A trial was held in 1834. Grier was acquitted on grounds of insanity. Though acquitted, Grier was enraged by the verdict that called his mental capabilities into question, and he published a pamphlet in an effort to explain why he had taken the law into his own hands. David Grier again proclaimed himself king of his mountain.

Convinced that the hermit was more than a nuisance, that he represented a threat to their lives and safety, the hermit's neighbors made numerous attempts on his life. Random rifle shots through his cabin door in the middle of the night were common. People were afraid of David Grier.

Grier did come down from his mountain long enough to find work in an iron forge, but he quickly proved he could not get along with people. He became involved in a dispute with a fellow worker, who turned out to be a relative of the hunter he had slain. Grier promised to kill this man, too, and to make good his threat before the day was over.

The ironworker was so fearful of David Grier, a known murderer, that he waited to ambush the hermit. When he saw the hermit returning from the mountain with his rifle, the ironworker killed David Grier.

So many had feared the hermit for so long that the killing of David Grier was interpreted as an act of self-defense. No charges were ever brought against the ironworker. It is not known where the hermit was buried, but his infamy lives on to this day to the extent that Big Bald Mountain is known as Grier's Bald by the people who live there, and to the extent that Grier's name still appears occasionally on maps of the mountains of western North Carolina.

THE PHANTOM CHOIR
OF THE ROAN
•••••••••••••
••

Not all ghosts are seen. Some are heard.

Many individuals—visitors and local residents alike—have heard the ghostly singing carried by the wind on Roan Mountain. Off Highway 261 in Mitchell County, bald Roan lies directly astride the North Carolina–Tennessee state line. Located in the northern half of the Pisgah National Forest, Roan Mountain rises to a majestic 6,285 feet, topped by a bald—an area in forested mountains where no trees grow. When topped by such a treeless peak, the mountain, too, is known as a bald.

Roan Mountain was claimed long ago by the Catawba Indians, who fought their battles there so that their dying warriors might be closer to the hand of the Great Father and so that the spirits of the sky, including thunder, lightning, wind, and rain, could better see their acts of bravery.

The Catawba once challenged all their enemies to come to Roan Mountain to battle for dominance in the Pisgah Forest. The Catawba defeated all those who came to fight in three drawn-out battles. The warring proved particularly gory, causing the letting of so much blood that pools and rivers of crimson withered the trees, which never grew back. Stained by the butchery, the rhododendron that has since taken hold at the edges of the bald on Roan Mountain is said to bloom a bright red.

The ghost choir of Roan Mountain is an old tale. Valley herdsmen believed that the song was merely the rushing sound of a natural wind, magnified by the configuration of rocks on Roan Mountain. However, the wind on Roan Mountain is anything but normal.

In 1799, John Strother, a member of the surveying team commissioned to establish the precise boundary between North Carolina and Tennessee, wrote in his diary of a wind that was so powerful that it "blowed deep holes all over the northwest side" of Roan Mountain. Farmers and area cattlemen spread the legend that it was the devil's wind that spun the clouds about the top of the mountain in a complete circle. Among other attributes, the wind was said to contain the voices of an otherworldly choir.

Those who hadn't heard the phantom music suggested that angels chose to practice their singing for Judgment Day above the Roan. Those who heard it knew otherwise. The phantom choir of Roan Mountain did not sing a joyful song, but a horrid, wretched song of mankind in torment. It was a baleful song that a bear caught in a trap might sing until the hunters came.

The view from bald Roan in any direction is fantastic. In 1878, a resort hotel was erected atop Roan Mountain by Colonel John Wilder to take advantage of the view. The building was situated so that guests were able to sleep in Tennessee and have breakfast in North Carolina without leaving the hotel.

The guests at Colonel Wilder's hotel were occasionally subjected to the haunting music of the evil wind, and word of its existence spread beyond the Pisgah Forest. Guests complained it was a savage wind that blew across Roan Mountain, that a stay in the mile-high hotel was like being locked in the hold of a ship upon a stormy sea. The hotel sometimes rocked and swayed in the wicked wind. The wind's song was said to be louder than a thousand humming bees encircling your head.

The hotel was failing when a man named Henry E. Colton visited Roan Mountain to seek the cause of the phantom music borne by the wind. Accompanied by Colonel Wilder and two others on an evening when the song was especially pronounced, Colton stood on the peak and did his best to analyze the noise by cocking his head from one side to the other and by taking a few quick steps this way, then that.

He described the experience for the Knoxville, Tennessee, newspaper. "The sound was very plain to the ear," Colton wrote. He described its most disturbing aspect as a rhythmic noise "like the incessant, continuous and combined snap of two glass jars" being tapped together. Colton dispelled the myth that the song was the humming of bees or flies by stating that the mysterious music was frequently heard "after the bees or flies had gone to their winter homes and before they came out again."

A man named Libourel, one of the younger guests at the hotel, told Colonel Wilder that he believed it was the devil's wind that had kept trees from growing at the top of Roan Mountain. On one particularly dark and gloomy day, the morning fog hanging low on the mountain and threatening to spend the entire day where it lay, the young guest resolved to discover the source of the wind and its song. He would, he believed, solve the mystery once and for all. Colonel Wilder warned him against the adventure and begged him to be cautious not to lose his way if he felt he must go out on his own. Colonel Wilder also told him that it would probably rain in the afternoon, as often happens on summer days in the mountains. The cocky visitor from out of state paid little heed to the warnings and left without preparing so much as a lunch or a canteen.

Guests who remembered seeing Libourel depart remarked that he wore dark blue pants and a plaid shirt. He carried a tree branch to use as a hiking stick.

Even a circular wind must have a source, Libourel thought. As the wind intensified, he believed he was nearing its origin. Then he heard the humming of ghostly voices in the wind. A thunderbolt rattled the sky, opening the dark clouds in a downpour.

Libourel was caught in a primeval force. Stumbling, he stopped at the edge of an outcropping of jagged rock, still clutching his walking stick. He took shelter in the crag's overhang by dropping to his hands and knees and crawling into the black wedge.

The velocity of the wind increased, tearing leaves from the branches of trees. For almost an hour he sat there, the humming taking over his senses.

The wind opened a cave at his back, or so it seemed. From this black hole came a shattering crescendo of wild howls. Perhaps the cave merely had gone unnoticed until that moment. Libourel could not be sure. He fell or was sucked backwards into the cave, hitting his head on a rock. Unconscious, he dreamed an unnatural dream. Or was he awake? It seemed to the young man that his eyes were closed. Whichever the case, he saw the ghostly choir of bald Roan.

The phantom singers were not the angels suggested by others. They were inhuman, though human forms they bore. Some were missing arms. Others had legs that were broken, their brittle bones exposed. All exhibited deep gashes in their flesh. Their singing was accompanied by a staccato of teeth inside their open mouths. Though most of the singers wore only their tattered flesh, bits of clothing clung to oozing places on one and another of the mournful horde. They definitely were not Indians killed in battle, Libourel realized, for one or two of the tortured singers wore manufactured shoes that were markedly different from the moccasins of American Indians.

The chorus was composed of beings from hell, Libourel was convinced. He was listening to the souls of the damned.

The awful music ceased after a time. The wind died. He climbed from the small cavern to discover that the rain had also stopped. The clouds had opened to reveal a blue sky.

At the southern edge of Roan Mountain's bald, the youthful Libourel, feeling older than mankind itself, witnessed what he believed to be a miracle and what many locals have claimed to see after hearing the music of the Roan. It was a rainbow. Blue, yellow, shimmering green, and red, it amazed him not only for its crisp colors. Like the clouds caught in Roan Mountain's circular wind, the rainbow was formed in a complete circle, a ring of blazing colors in the sky.

Area residents who swear they have seen such a rainbow over Roan Mountain refer to it as "God's halo." Had Libourel witnessed heaven battling back the winds of hell? The young man grasped his stick tightly in both hands and hurried back to the hotel. Without speaking a word to anyone, he packed his belongings and paid his bill, then promptly left the mountain for good.

Guests who'd seen Libourel after his adventure remarked upon his disheveled appearance. When he'd returned to the resort, his dark blue pants were pure white and his plaid shirt was as white as a bleached sheet, its buttons missing. The stick he'd carried with him was utterly bare, having been cleanly stripped of its bark. Many believed it was the wind that had blown the colors from his clothes, the same wind that carries the song of the phantom choir of Roan Mountain.

It was years after the resort hotel had been torn down that Libourel, safe in his home back east, managed to bring himself to speak of his experiences on Roan Mountain. He claimed to his death that those who thought the music of Roan Mountain was a chorus of angels were badly mistaken. Locals who purported such a tale had never heard the terrible music, he claimed. And to this day those who witness the occasional appearance of a circular rainbow over the Roan cannot imagine the beauty of such a sight to the eyes of one who crawled out of a frightful cave and looked heavenward to see what could only be the halo of God Himself.

Today, visitors to Roan Mountain may still locate the row of stones that formed the foundation of Colonel Wilder's resort hotel. It is advised that neither children nor adults attempt to find a small cave under an outcropping of rock at the edge of the bald. There are worse fates than getting caught in an afternoon mountain rain.

TILL DEATH DO YOU PART
. . . .
. .

Begun in the 1930s, the Blue Ridge Parkway connects the Shenandoah National Park in Virginia to the Great Smoky Mountains National Park at the far edge of the Cherokee Indian reservation in North Carolina, all without a single stop sign. The 470-mile parkway was completed in 1987 with the construction of the Linn Cove Viaduct, which curves spectacularly around 5,964-foot Grandfather Mountain just north of Linville. Said to be a billion years old, Grandfather Mountain is a rock formation that appears to profile an old man lying in repose.

It was in the shadow of Grandfather Mountain, among the abundant rhododendrons, azaleas, mountain laurels, and red spruces, that Malinda Coffey Pritchard pledged her loyalty and devotion to L. McKesson "Keith" Blalock upon a wedding altar in 1856.

McKesson Blalock was given the nickname of Keith out of respect for his physical prowess. Locals claimed he was as fierce a fighter as Alfred Keith, an aging mountain man over in Burnsville. Keith Blalock's fists were claimed to be as big as hams and as hard as rocks. Yet it was his gun and the loyalty of his wife that earned the ruffian Keith Blalock his fame—and infamy—during the War Between the States.

You must remember that many of the mountain people in western North Carolina were not in favor of the Confederacy. Though a definite minority, these Union sympathizers were often quite vocal. The mountain Unionists proved themselves fiercely independent, operating a pipeline for Union loyalists who slipped across the state line in small numbers to join Federal forces operating in Tennessee.

Many desperate men, deserters from both the Union and Confederate armies, poured into the rugged regions of western North Carolina because it was a good place to hide and because people who lived there were known to help those from either side. Indeed, even some households were divided, with family members providing refuge for men on the run from both Union and Confederate forces.

During the six years before the War Between the States, Malinda and Keith Blalock shared a cabin in Avery County near the town of Montezuma. Keith sympathized with the Union cause, but as a local resident he was unable to escape the conscript law of the Confederacy. Of sound mind and body, he was subject to the draft.

Keith decided that his only course of action was to enlist in the Confederate army. He may have planned to slip across enemy lines or to operate as a Union spy. Neither opportunity would be afforded him by his brothers in gray.

Malinda threw a fit. Under no circumstances would she be left behind when Keith joined the Twenty-sixth Regiment of the Army of the Confederate States of America. Malinda had the will and she found the way.

She changed her name to Sam. She fashioned herself a pair of men's trousers, a shirt, and a jacket. Then Malinda chopped off her hair and joined the Confederate army with her husband, passing muster as Keith's younger brother.

Many believe that Malinda's deceit was the height of loyalty to her husband, that she couldn't tolerate spending a night without him. More likely, it was the couple's plan to desert the Confederacy together.

Malinda's disguise worked. "Sam" Blalock was issued a ball-and-cap musket and a gray wool uniform with brass buttons. She tented with her brother and took her turn standing guard. She drilled alongside the other soldiers and was said to handle her musket as well as any man. In short, she excelled at soldiery, and no one suspected that Sam Blalock was a woman.

The Twenty-sixth was posted at Kinston, North Carolina, far from Federal lines. Once it became apparent that their chances of contact with Union troops were slim for the duration of their duty at Kinston, Keith came up with another plan. He slipped away from guard duty and into the nearby woods one day. There he sought out a patch of poison oak and, stripping bare, rubbed the leaves over his entire body. Within a day, his skin was badly inflamed.

Professing a fever of unknown origins, displaying an angry rash that might be contagious, Keith Blalock received a medical discharge from the Confederate army. The discharge was granted with the understanding that should he become well, he would reenlist. Sam had a bit of a problem, however, in joining her husband in his newfound freedom.

Her disguise had worked too well. Upon hearing Sam's confession, her commanding officer refused to believe she was a woman. Whatever physical evidence Malinda had to offer is best left to the imagination. Suffice it to say that she was able to convince those in charge that she was indeed a woman.

John W. Moore's *Roster of the North Carolina Troops in the War Between the States* does, in fact, list both Blalocks among the active members of the Twenty-sixth Regiment. Malinda is boldly listed as "Mrs. L. M. Blalock," with the following notation: "Discharged for being a woman. This lady had done a soldier's duty without a suspicion of her sex among her comrades until her husband, L. M. Blalock, was discharged, when she claimed the same privilege and was sent home."

Troubles weren't over for the Blalocks or their mountain neighbors.

After Keith Blalock was "cured," the Confederacy offered him a choice between reenlisting and being branded a traitor. Keith wanted no more of the gray army, and he fled with his wife to live in a hut in the wild recesses of Grandfather Mountain. He and Malinda were said to be living off wild game. No doubt, Keith shot and butchered an occasional deer, rabbit, and squirrel.

Loyal Confederates living in the area told a different story of how Keith Blalock brought home the bacon. Other deserters had apparently joined the Blalocks on Grandfather Mountain, creating a small colony of vicious outlaws known as the Blalock Gang. Many a farmer's pig and cow and many a grandmother's hen mysteriously disappeared during this period.

It wasn't long before Confederate recruiters came after the gang, which dispersed after a shoot-out that resulted in Keith's being hit in the left arm by a rifle ball. The Blalocks and a few of their cohorts hightailed it to the Tennessee mountains, it is believed. Soon, though, they returned—with a vengeance.

Never one to avoid a fight, Keith set about bushwhacking the residents of western North Carolina with the rest of his gang. He was often seen wearing a blue coat of the Union army. With Union military marauder George W. Kirk in the saddle, the gang created turmoil in the area of Grandfather Mountain. Sweeping down on horseback from wooded hideouts, they robbed, plundered, and destroyed. Just as she had joined her husband when he enlisted in the Confederate army, Malinda galloped her own steed alongside Keith in a number of these raids. No man dared walk unarmed through the mountains.

When the Blalock Gang attacked a Confederate home in Globe, North Carolina, they were repulsed, but not before Malinda was wounded in the shoulder. Keith swore revenge for the fracas that he had instigated, but in a subsequent skirmish with the same family, he lost an eye. It was a lucky shot from the gun of one of the family's sons who was too young to enlist in the war effort.

The War Between the States ended, but the Blalocks had discovered a way of life that was difficult to put aside. The gang continued to ride, feuding with those they had bullied and robbed. There were old scores to settle, as far as Keith was concerned. In February of 1866, he culminated one feud by charging out of the bushes along a country path and shooting one John Boyd. Boyd fell dead on the spot. Although there was a witness to the murder, Unionist Governor W. W. Holden inexplicably pardoned Keith Blalock.

Eventually, the Blalocks settled into a more peaceful routine. Keith drew a Union pension for wounded veterans and even ran for a seat on the state legislature. He was defeated. Malinda died in 1901. In 1913, at the age of seventy-seven, one-eyed Keith Blalock was killed when the railroad handcar he was operating plunged from the track on a steep mountain curve.

The name Blalock is still recognized by locals in the Grandfather Mountain area. Despised by many, Keith Blalock continues to be associated with the violence and misery of the War Between the States as it was fought in the mountainous region of western North Carolina. The lives of Keith and Malinda recall a desperate period of gang attacks, cavalry raids, and illegal destruction.

CULGEE WATSON'S
SUNDAY CLOTHES
•••••••••••••
••

Some mountain people are remembered for their ruggedness or
their independence. Their names survive because they embodied
a spirit still prevalent among many who choose to live in the wild
outback of the North Carolina mountains.

In the past, visitors were advised to approach mountain homes
with caution. No Trespassing signs were to be taken seriously. On
evenings of humid weather, families moved their furniture out of
their cabins and into their yards. A family's yard became an
extension of the home, and walking across a mountain yard
unannounced was the equivalent of walking into a city neighbor's
house without knocking. Stepping onto the porch of an isolated
mountain home without an invitation was the same as sneaking
into someone's bedroom. And a mountain home was likely to
have a shotgun handy just inside the door.

As a matter of both courtesy and self-protection, mountain
settlers in western North Carolina developed the custom of
hollering hello. A would-be visitor stood at the edge of a cabin's

clearing and, putting both hands to his mouth, yelled to ask if anyone was home. Someone would step out onto the porch, and the visitor, if he was known, would be invited to approach.

If there was no reply, the visitor simply made his call another day. In good weather, mountain residents were usually out working somewhere among the forested glens—tending cattle, feeding geese, keeping bees—so a visitor's holler was as likely to be answered from beyond the nearby trees as from the cabin itself. Approaching a home without announcing your presence was taken as an attempt to rob the cabin.

Tourists who explore the many unmarked, twisting roads of the North Carolina mountains are advised to follow this custom even today. It should be remembered that many people who take to the rugged outback are hermits who may not welcome company for a variety of reasons. They may choose to ignore a holler and wait patiently for a visitor to walk away and leave them alone.

Culgee Watson was one such hermit, and a colorful eccentric to boot. He took up residence on Gingercake Mountain in the late 1700s and is believed to be the man who gave the mountain its name.

Rising to four thousand feet, Gingercake is named for the unique stack of rocks on its summit. One huge boulder, eight feet thick and thirty-two feet long, is delicately balanced on a thirty-foot-tall pyramid-shaped stone called Sitting Bear Rock. The balanced slab of granite looks as light as a slice of ginger cake, but it is impossible to stand underneath it without a feeling of pronounced insecurity—surely the slightest breeze will cause it to fall, though geologists insist that the formation has existed since the retreat of the Ice Age.

Gingercake Mountain is part of Jonas Ridge, which forms the eastern edge of Linville Gorge in northern Burke County, one of the most dramatic canyons in the Blue Ridge Mountains. Trees grow improbably out of the walls of the gorge, and rhododendrons and hemlocks are in abundance, as is rainfall.

Culgee Watson's life before he came to Gingercake Mountain is a mystery that died with the hermit in 1816. He was noted for his friendliness to wild and domesticated animals and to other men, but there was one thing he could not stand.

He hated women.

It was rumored that Culgee had suffered a grand disappointment in love, and that this was perhaps the reason he found his way to the backwoods to live the life of a hermit. Whatever the case, he was never heard to speak a word to a woman after moving to Gingercake Mountain. Unkind neighbors claimed he was simply "tetched in the haid."

Though considered harmless, Culgee went to great extremes to protect himself from the presence of the fair sex whenever they wandered unknowingly near his small, two-room log cabin in the woods. He built a tall fence of split rails around his yard. Culgee hated women so strongly that he would burn a rail of his fence should any woman so much as lean upon it to holler a hello in the direction of his cabin. From his hiding place, Culgee peered out to watch the occasional woman approach and leave his yard unanswered. Then he went to work. Besides burning any portion of his fence the woman touched, Culgee threw scoops of dirt upon the places where her shoes had touched the ground. He also turned the earth with a shovel wherever any woman had sat to take a rest on his property.

Culgee Watson loved peacocks as much as he hated women. Raising peacocks was both his major occupation and favorite recreation. Culgee's neighbors realized he had little trouble making ends meet, and it was generally assumed that he had brought to the mountains enough money to get by on for the rest of his life.

Culgee found peacocks to be superior watchdogs. At the approach of intruders, their screeching was more effective than a dog's barking. They served ample warning whenever anyone, especially a woman, approached his cabin yard.

The peacocks also provided Culgee with the adornments of his most colorful eccentricity. His remarkable taste in fashion featured clothes he made himself, decorated with the brilliantly colored feathers of his male peacocks. All the garments Culgee made were trimmed with the feathers of his watchdog peacocks. We can only guess what his birds may have thought when Culgee strutted around his yard dressed as one of them. But his reputation as a flashy dresser spread quickly among the mountain folk.

The hermit's favorite suit was topped off by a coat that was covered with the iridescent spots and shimmering colors of its stitched-on peacock feathers. When a mountain man dressed up in his best suit, he was said to be putting on his Sunday clothes. People in the area referred to the suit as "Culgee Watson's Sunday clothes."

The hermit had another name for his favorite coat of lustrous splendor. He referred to it as his "culgee."

Neighbors, including those who suspected the hermit was attempting to learn to fly, never discovered why Watson called his coat a culgee. No one had ever heard the word before, but the name caught on and the hermit was soon known by everyone in the mountains as Culgee Watson. To this day, his real first name is a mystery.

Culgee's feathered clothes were his own worst enemy. They attracted onlookers. Because of the flamboyant display of the "Birdman of Gingercake," many people, including women, traveled from far and wide to his fenced-in yard and called to the hermit to come out so they could see his culgee. This, no doubt, contributed to his abundant supply of firewood, as the hermit continued to remove and destroy any portion of his fence touched by a woman.

Perhaps it was the North Carolina mountain custom of hollering hello that kept poor Culgee Watson from having to burn down his entire cabin. No woman was ever known to set foot on his porch or lay a knock upon his door until after his death. And maybe, just maybe, if the hermit had located his fashion center in Paris rather than in the isolated Blue Ridge Mountains outback, we'd all be wearing peacock feathers.

BELINDA AND THE
BROWN MOUNTAIN LIGHTS
•••••••••••••
••

There's nothing scarier than a mountain at night.

When the thick summer leaves of western North Carolina's towering trees block out even the light of the brightest full moon, the ground itself disappears in front of your feet, though you know you must be walking on *something*. The whole world around you becomes black shadow upon black shade.

While scientists insist the human eye is capable of distinguishing forty shades of gray, you'd swear in the woods at night there are a hundred variations of black. A black that is a darkness against an even dimmer black, then a black that is blacker than that, and another black chasing after still another. A spiderweb is a thing of terror, and every shadow is a snake.

Walking through a mountain forest at night among the multiple shapes, each darker than obscurity itself, you can hear your heartbeat, feel your own breath move across your face. Reaching out to feel your way is a mistake. You want very badly not to touch anything, and you want just as badly to have nothing touch you.

The best way to get through a night in the mountains without a light is to find a smooth rock at dusk and sit there without moving until daylight. Unknown things will be moving around you, of course. Noises will haunt your imagination and your reason alike. Noises that might be bears rustling nearby leaves or twigs snapping under the padded feet of a mountain panther will test your sanity. Going insane is probably better than falling off a cliff or stumbling into the quiet, deep water of a mountain pool.

Pioneers who explored the wooded mountains valued clearings. They cut down trees, while the Indians sought out natural clearings from which they seldom strayed at night. Fire was needed at night for light as much as for heat. Even though it might attract undesirable wildlife, the summer fire was stoked through many moonless forest nights.

It is little wonder that any light brighter than a star attracted the awe and suspicion of people in the mountains. It is little wonder, even in this day of electricity, lanterns, and flashlights, that many people travel to catch a glimpse of the mysterious and unexplained Brown Mountain Lights.

Usually visible on partly cloudy nights when the moon is a slim slice or is hidden by the clouds altogether, the Brown Mountain Lights are colorful globes that rise in the sky over northern Burke County, North Carolina. The lights have been sighted singularly and in groups. They range in color from yellow to blood red, and have even been reported in a ghostly shade of blue.

The first documented sighting of the lights was in 1771, when Gerard William de Brahm, a German engineer visiting the area, wrote that Brown Mountain emitted a nitrous vapor which was borne by the wind. He went on to explain that the wind caused the nitrous vapor to inflame, creating the mysterious lights. Brahm's explanation of the phenomenon turned out to be inaccurate.

Cherokee Indians from the area suggest the lights were seen by their ancestors many generations prior to Brahm's mountain visit. In the thirteenth century, long before the arrival of any white man, the Cherokee and Catawba fought a fierce battle at the base of Brown Mountain.

It was a generation after this battle that the lights began to appear, according to Cherokee legend. The Brown Mountain Lights are the spirits of Indian maidens—long dead—searching for the spirits of their husbands, brothers, and fathers who were killed during the battle and whose souls were lost beyond the reach of the Great Father.

While a body of folktales has grown up around the Brown Mountain Lights, it should be pointed out that no scientific explanation for the appearance of the lights exists. Unimpressive as far as mountains go, Brown Mountain rises to but twenty-six hundred feet and is best described as a long, low ridge when viewed from higher points in Burke and Avery counties.

Numerous sightings of the strange lights have been documented over the years, and the lights are still visible today from vantage points along the Blue Ridge Parkway and from points between Blowing Rock and Linville.

Margaret Jordan of the *Davenport Weekly Record* of Lenoir, North Carolina, wrote in April of 1922 that "the mysterious light on Brown Mountain . . . has again been seen by the Burke County people." She went on to recount one of the first attempts to explain the lights, noting that on June 8, 1908, "a body of men was immediately dispatched from Morganton to learn the cause of the light, but the expedition was a failure."

Those curious men from Morganton shouldn't have felt too badly, even though they trooped over to Brown Mountain again three nights later when the light was spotted once more. Every scientific attempt since then to explain the appearance of the ghostly Brown Mountain Lights has failed.

In 1913, a United States Geological Survey investigation verified that the lights did indeed exist. After a brief examination, the investigators determined that the lights were nothing more than the reflected headlights of trains traveling through the Catawba Valley at the base of Brown Mountain.

The locals knew that there was not a chance that this was true. The lights had been seen long before the coming of trains to the area. A severe flooding of the Catawba Valley in 1916 proved them right. The flood washed away railroad tracks and bridges and tore down power poles in the valley. Throughout the weeks it took to restore the tracks, the Brown Mountain Lights continued to appear regularly. The flood was nature's way of disproving the scientists who attempted to write off one of her mysteries as another matter of routine reason.

Later in the decade, the United States Geological Survey again investigated the mystery lights, this time along with the United States Weather Bureau. Using a wide array of modern instruments, they determined that lights appearing above the mountain arose from the spontaneous combustion of marsh gasses. They also suggested that any remaining lights were the reflections of brush fires.

Marsh gasses? Perhaps they were paying too much attention to their instruments and ignoring their surroundings. There are no marshy areas on or anywhere near Brown Mountain, no swampy holes where such gasses might gather.

It didn't take other scientists long to discount this theory. It was noted that phosphorous combustion could not have been seen from great distances even if marsh gasses were present; phosphorous combustion is more visible as you approach its origin. The Brown Mountain Lights, on the other hand, seem to disappear as you approach, and they are rarely visible at all from lower altitudes, where swamp gas would be likely to accumulate. Again, the lights are seen high above Brown Mountain.

In a 1940 report, Hobart A. Whitman concluded that the lights were not the result of natural ground sources. He analyzed rocks and soil from Brown Mountain and the surrounding area for any unusual elements. The rocks and soil didn't differ from rocks and soil across the entire western region of North Carolina.

As for brush fires, the mountain would have long ago burned down to support so many fires for so many years.

The Smithsonian Institution discounted the popular theory that the Brown Mountain Lights were a manifestation of St. Elmo's fire, the electric-glow phenomenon occurring at the edge of a solid conductor such as an airplane wing. St. Elmo's fire does not occur in midsky as do the Brown Mountain Lights.

Eventually, it was suggested that the lights were a mirage, the best scientific explanation of the regular appearance of the mysterious, floating globes over Brown Mountain to date. Legend has taken over where science failed. If the lights cannot be explained by science, they must exist outside the world of science.

Unexplained lights at night are often personified in folklore and Indian legend as a lover in search of his or her beloved in the eternal hereafter. This is true of the Brown Mountain Lights as well. One legend has it that a storm swept away a beau on his scheduled night of elopement; his faithful lover waits still with a lantern in her hand for his arrival. Another version has it that a lover burns a candle as she searches for her beloved, who was murdered by a jealous rival.

An interesting explanation of the Brown Mountain Lights was popular among early lumberjacks in the area, hardy souls who spent every hour of daylight cutting the tall trees of the western North Carolina forests. The story spread among them that the mysterious colored lights were the reflection of the moon off a rare gem somewhere on the mountain's face. Rubies are, in fact, to be found throughout the North Carolina mountains. One will never know, however, how many lumberjacks searched in darkness for a gem clear and powerful enough to reflect light from the moon.

When you perch on a ledge at dusk to watch the darkness creep up the valleys and overtake the mountains, one story of the Brown Mountain Lights is likely to send a chill up your spine. If you stand in the descending darkness to see the mountain better, this explanation seems as real as the buzzing of July insects in the cluster of trees and shrubbery at your back. It's the story of Belinda.

Before the War Between the States, mountain marriages were made when a man and a woman decided to live together. So it was that Belinda, still a teenager and expecting a baby, was married to Jim. According to his sister's granddaughter, Jim was cruel. The story of his cruelty still circulates today.

As the birth of his child approached, Jim grew meaner yet. It was also known in the area around Brown Mountain, where the couple shared a cabin, that Jim was seeing another woman, known only as Susie.

Jim was crazy about Susie. He couldn't do enough to please her. Nor could he have been any nastier to Belinda. Belinda, by all accounts, was a good, trusting woman, sincere in her effort to be a wife and a mother in the rugged mountain country.

As Susie and Jim plotted his freedom, Belinda stuck it out. There's no telling how many nights she spent alone in the cold cabin surrounded by the frightening noises of a mountain night, and there's no counting the number of times she was beaten by Jim for a crime no greater than conceiving his child.

On the day she gave birth, Belinda disappeared. A neighbor heard the cries of the newborn while tending cattle allowed to roam freely on the hillside near Jim and Belinda's small cabin. Yet neither Belinda nor the child was seen or heard from again.

Area folks, including members of Belinda's and Jim's families, approached the young father about the disappearance of his wife.

To hear Jim tell it, there was no baby. He is said to have stood in his doorway, barring entry to the cabin. He scratched his head and said his wife had put on her bonnet one day last week and taken off.

"And no, she ain't come back yet."

No one believed his feeble tale. People from the area began to search for the young woman. A relative of Belinda's found her bonnet several miles from the cabin door. There was dried blood on the bonnet, according to reports. As searchers concentrated their efforts in the wooded area where the bonnet was found, a fire broke out. The entire woods was burned, destroying any further evidence of foul play. Those who didn't care for Jim—and there were plenty—believed he had set the fire.

The bloodied bonnet was not enough to convince the constable that Jim had murdered his wife. Belinda might have been scratched by a thornbush as she walked away from her home, or some evil other than Jim might have come her way. Still, many believed Jim had found a way to rid himself of the family he'd begun before meeting Susie.

About the time of the fire, Susie moved into the cabin with Jim, and the mysterious lights over Brown Mountain began to appear.

At first, the locals simply watched their colorful display night after night. One by one, they became convinced that the eerie lights meant something, that there was a reason for their existence. Two elderly women, concerned about the missing wife and the rumor that her baby had been born, followed the lights one evening, walking through undergrowth and bramblebush and carrying oil-burning lanterns, until they were directly under the brightest of the glowing orbs of changing color. There, they found a pile of stones at the bottom of a high cliff. They unpiled the stones the next morning and discovered the skulls of a grown person and a baby.

There is a myth in the mountains that the skull of a murder victim never decays, and that it remains intact for a reason. When the skull is held aloft over the head of the murderer, the murderer cannot tell a lie about the crime.

The skulls were carried to Jim's cabin right away. While Susie was kept at bay by the older women, one of whom was her aunt, Jim was held in his chair by two strong men and asked if he'd killed his wife and baby. Another man held both skulls over his head.

Jim was unable to speak a word in his defense, so he chose not to speak at all. It was reported that he turned ghostly white and began to tremble, afraid to say anything. In fact, he never said another word as long as he lived.

Jim may not have lived all that long. It's unclear what happened to him. Some say he went insane, hollering meaningless mono-syllables and beating Susie until she left him in fear of her life. Some say a strange illness overtook him and he died shortly thereafter. Others suggest that mountain justice was served by the hands of honest men, including Belinda's brother. Mountain people were known to keep a stony silence when it came to discussing the fate of evildoers "taken care of" in this way.

Many believe that the Brown Mountain Lights exist for a purpose. The descendants of the families of Belinda, Susie, and Jim—some of whom still live in the area—believe that the lights are the ghosts of Belinda and her unnamed baby, showing the searchers where their bodies were hidden.

At mile marker 310 on the Blue Ridge Parkway, a turnout at an elevation of 3,805 feet at Lost Cove Cliffs affords a view of Brown Mountain and, on the right nights, a glimpse of the eerie, unexplained Brown Mountain Lights.

Locals prefer driving to Linville Falls and then taking the United States Forest Service road to Wiseman's View. From this lookout, the lights appear larger and brighter than stars. Some observers have described the lights as fiery, colored balls like those shot from a Roman candle. By all accounts, the lights do move around a bit, even to the point of "zooming."

Wiseman's View offers a favorite vista in the North Carolina mountains even in daylight, including mountain gorges and rising highlands nearly as dramatic as the Brown Mountain Lights themselves. A parking area has been improved recently, and well-maintained trails lead to lookouts complete with safety rails and numerous places to spread a blanket. Just in case you lose your flashlight, you'll have a comfortable place to sit out the night.

A LOVER LIVES
TO LEAP AGAIN
•••••••••••
••

According to *Ripley's Believe It or Not*, there's only one place in the world where the snow falls upside down.

That place is Blowing Rock, one of the oldest resorts in the mountains and one of North Carolina's favorite postcards, located where the Blue Ridge Parkway enters the northern edge of the Pisgah National Forest in Watauga County.

It's a romantic spot, particularly when the thick mist characteristic of the Blue Ridge Mountains overflows the steep valleys. The soft clouds invite you to leap from the edge of the mountainside cliff because you are sure that the clouds will lower you safely to the valley floor 3,586 feet below.

Blowing Rock is named for the rock formation that overhangs the Johns River Valley. The rocky walls of the gorge form a funnel, and the southwest wind often sweeps up the canyon wall with some force. Light objects, such as scarves and caps, are sometimes returned to their owners when cast over the void.

Legend has it that words of love whispered from Blowing Rock are carried on the mysterious wind to one's object of devotion anywhere in the world. It was this rising wind that inspired Robert L. Ripley's cartoon. During a light snow, flakes may actually be seen falling upside down as they rise from the valley to the sky above Blowing Rock.

The wind, in another way, is said to have helped create Blowing Rock as a successful resort town when in 1875 William Morris began to take in summer boarders. Mrs. Morris was an exceptional cook. The aromas of her baked goods were carried by the rising wind across the fertile fields of the North Carolina Piedmont to the east. Some were said to have followed their noses to the mountain village from as far away as the Atlantic coast. Senator M. W. Ransom was so fond of Mrs. Morris's cooking that he built a summer home in Blowing Rock that started a trend. Soon the mountainous area was dotted with inns and summer homes.

Two variations of a Cherokee legend account for the wind at Blowing Rock. The Cherokee were the greatest and most far-reaching nation of American Indians, and the only one to have its own alphabet and written language. Cherokee still occupy a reservation at the southeastern edge of the Great Smoky Mountains National Park. The Blue Ridge Parkway passes through the reservation just north of the town of Cherokee.

The Cherokee in the Smoky Mountains of western North Carolina are descendants of a group that fled from General Winfield Scott's soldiers in 1838 during the so-called Indian removal, also known as the Trail of Tears. Cherokee legends of western North Carolina are perhaps as rich and numerous as those from any other region in their ancient territory.

In the Cherokee world, numerous gods were at work in the forces of nature, all under the rule of one Great Father. Two of these gods play prominent roles in the surviving legends of

Blowing Rock. Regretfully, Anglo adaptions cannot be separated from the original Indian myths, and we are able only to relate the legends as they exist today. Suffice it to say that Victorian America has colored the legends of Blowing Rock. It is our hope that the spirit of the original Cherokee myth is contained in the following legends.

Love is the driving force behind the Indian legends of Blowing Rock. In each, a lovely daughter's coming of age is at the heart of the story.

Her name was Wenonah, which means "firstborn daughter." The Indians knew her as Daughter of the Stars, Princess Starlight, or Little Starlight. Whichever the translation, it is apparent that Wenonah was quite attractive, and that she grew even more so as her girl's body grew into a woman's.

Wenonah was the daughter of Osseo, a powerful elder who governed a vast and rich domain in which game, fruit, and corn were all abundant. Osseo held influence over the other Indians in his region and was a very wealthy man. Like all good fathers, he loved his beautiful daughter above all else.

It was with sorrow that Osseo faced Wenonah's physical blossoming. Reluctantly, he did the correct thing, sending messengers carrying willow branches to all the camps in the Cherokee Nation. The willow was a sign that his much-adored daughter was ready for marriage and that Osseo had agreed she could receive suitors.

Young men, along with a few older fellows, rushed at once to offer themselves as Wenonah's husband. Gifts were presented and feats were performed in an effort to gain the favor of both Wenonah and her father. Among the Cherokee, father and daughter must agree before a marriage can take place.

The older suitors recounted acts of bravery, each insisting that he could best provide for and protect this Daughter of the Stars, while the younger men engaged in graceful displays of dance or played the prettiest songs on reed instruments. The decision was a difficult one for Wenonah and Osseo.

It is at this point the legend breaks into two separate tales.

In the more romantic version, Wenonah was unable to decide between two young men who were both acceptable as future husbands, and the two men fought to determine who would move into her home. They wrestled each other in a series of daring and desperate holds along the narrow cliffs above the Johns River. One of the strong young men lost purchase and fell screaming from a precipice into the valley far below.

Upon hearing his echoing scream, Wenonah realized it was the fallen man she was meant to marry.

In the more realistic version, Osseo and Wenonah agreed that one particular suitor should become her husband. He was Kwasind, a singer who had traveled many miles to perform for Wenonah. Kwasind was also handsome and very strong.

Before the marriage could be consummated, however, a rival suitor whose offer of marriage had been shunned told Wenonah that Kwasind was already married, that he had left behind a wife in a distant valley who would one day come looking for him. The story was a lie, but Wenonah believed it. She loved Kwasind and considered him the perfect man for her, but the revelation of his alleged marriage made her distraught with the pain and rage of jealousy. Finally, Wenonah confronted Kwasind on a cliff and told him that she would rather see him dead than marry him.

"Without you," he said, "my life is of no value." Kwasind then leapt from an outcropping of rock high above the Johns River.

In both cases, the man Wenonah loved fell to his apparent death. And in both cases, she realized that a horrible mistake had been made while her beloved was still in midair.

Wenonah tore at her clothes and, sobbing, threw herself to the ground. She prayed out loud to the gods who had been kindest to her family, the god of the west wind and the god of the south wind. The gods heard the maiden's plea and were moved by her anguish. Together, the two winds combined to lift the doomed man from his descent, returning him to the exact spot from which he'd fallen. He alighted intact on Blowing Rock and lifted Wenonah from the ground in a strong embrace.

Wenonah spent the rest of her life in happiness, each day thanking the two gods who'd saved her husband. In turn, the gods were so pleased with Wenonah's thankfulness that they continued to lift the wind straight up from the Johns River Gorge to the sky above Blowing Rock.

It is difficult to stand at Blowing Rock and view the floor of the steep valley below without thinking of the faith of Wenonah, without wishing that somewhere in the world there were a wind strong enough to lift you up to rebound like starlight from your irredeemable mistakes.

The authors invite your comments. You may write to them in care of

John F. Blair, Publisher
1406 Plaza Drive
Winston-Salem, NC 27103.

ABOUT THE AUTHORS

Randy Russell and Janet Barnett first visited the North Carolina mountains on their honeymoon. They returned to their home in Kansas City, Missouri, with an inspiration to collect some of the mountain legends that they had discovered.

Barnett, who helps to organize the world of computers at a Kansas City hospital, acted as a research assistant while Russell slaved over a typewriter to produce this collection. Russell is a free-lance writer whose poetry has been published in several journals including the *Paris Review* and *Kansas Quarterly*. His two detective mysteries are scheduled to be published by Bantam Books in 1989.

A NOTE ON THE TYPE

The text of this book was set in Perpetua, a typestyle designed and introduced in 1932 by Eric Gill. Its form is based on inscriptional letters of old style appearance with clean, engraved strokes and needle-fine serifs.

Composed by Superior Typesetters, Inc.
Winston-Salem, North Carolina

Printed and bound by
R. R. Donnelley & Sons Company, Harrisonburg, Virginia

Book design by
DEBRA HAMPTON